NINJA WARFARE

Natty's weapon was out of ammunition. The ninja grinned as he pulled a six-pointed star from his sleeve. The deadly steel blades of the shuriken had been dipped in a neurotoxic poison that would kill Natty Tracker in seconds. Tracker waited calmly, watching the pupil of the assassin's eye. When it dilated, he would have one quarter second to react.

The ninja's pupil flared. Natty threw the empty machine pistol into the assassin's eye, diving forward in an attack somersault. The deadly poisoned star sailed harmlessly over Tracker's head . . .

The TRACKER Series by Ron Stillman

TRACKER
TRACKER 2: GREEN LIGHTNING

TRACKER 3: BLOOD MONEY
(coming in March!)

TRACKER
GREEN LIGHTNING
RON STILLMAN

CHARTER/DIAMOND BOOKS, NEW YORK

GREEN LIGHTNING

A Charter/Diamond Book / published by arrangement with
the author

PRINTING HISTORY
Charter/Diamond edition / December 1990

All rights reserved.
Copyright © 1990 by Charter Communications, Inc.
This book may not be reproduced in whole or in part, by
mimeograph or any other means, without permission. For
information address: The Berkley Publishing Group, 200
Madison Avenue, New York, New York 10016.

ISBN: 1-55773-426-7

Charter/Diamond Books are published by The Berkley Publishing Group, 200 Madison Avenue, New York, New York 10016.
The name "CHARTER/DIAMOND" and its logo are trademarks belonging to Charter Communications, Inc.

PRINTED IN THE UNITED STATES OF AMERICA

10 9 8 7 6 5 4 3 2 1

1.

Assassin

LOOKING AT HER from behind in the darkened room, you could see the muscular shape of her calf muscles as she bent over and pulled the nylon stocking up her right leg. It slid noiselessly over the well-shaped, shaven, and waxed leg, and she clipped it at mid-thigh to the black lace garter belt. The black bikini briefs anchored her smooth muscular back, partially hidden in shadow. Over her athletic shoulders hung beautiful curly brown hair highlighted by slivers of moonlight streaking through the deserted building's skylight. The hair was naturally curly and cut in a tuxedo shag. From the rear, she appeared well-shaped and sexy.

The woman turned, and her face was illuminated by light flooding in from a streetlamp outside the dirty window. The brown eyes were intense, very intense. She ran her hands up and down each stockinged leg, smoothing the nylons. She looked at her hairdo in the mirror and carefully brushed back her soft tresses with her fingers. She twisted at the waist and looked at the back of her dress in the mirror to see if it fell properly. The hemline touched the back of her legs a few inches above the knees. Her hands reached down and felt the material as it fell over her buttocks.

Satisfied, she turned back and looked at her face in the mirror and splashed warm water on it. She looked at the dark arched eyebrows and the piercing brown, almost black, eyes. Her eyes drifted down to her nose while she placed a little shaving cream below it.

Below the broken nose was a dark Pancho Villa-type moustache. He raised a Gillette Trac II razor to it and quickly removed it with several strokes.

His name was Miguel Atencio, and he was the best in the world at his job: killing people. He had been hired by an electronic oriental mafia called the Ryoku Rai Kyookai, which translates as the Green Lightning Society. The "green" stood for money and the "lightning" stood for the use of electronics and computers. Miguel's pay was a cool ten million dollars, and he was to assassinate the President of the United States in the most expedient manner and at the earliest possible time.

The reason the RRK wanted the President dead was because he had been around Washington a long time, had a great deal of leadership, and an administration with an apparent abundance of competence.

As the late author Louis L'Amour used to say, "He had been over the mountains and down the river."

GREEN LIGHTNING

The Vice President, on the other hand, was relatively young and inexperienced with only a fraction of the President's political savvy. The RRK strongly desired a less powerful political infrastructure in the Washington bureaucracy and felt this could be achieved with the popular President out of the way. The ten million offered to Atencio for that task was only a drop in the bucket to these modern-day robber barons and was considered well worth the risk.

A jock and a sports fan, the President had decided to attend a football game between the arch-rival Denver Broncos and Cleveland Browns at Cleveland Stadium, while he was in Cleveland for political functions. The game was to be televised on ABC's "Monday Night Football," so it would take place at night; so would the assassination.

Dressed as a fashionable young lady, Miguel Atencio would be seated a good distance from the President's box and entourage, and he would effect the hit with a stolen US Army M-79 grenade launcher. When the Cleveland fans started yelling from the Dawg Pound and the rest of the bleachers, he would quickly start firing grenades into the area of the President's box. Miguel would move in the confusion to a maintenance closet, for which he had already stolen a key, and change from his dress into a man's outfit and move to another seat elsewhere in the stadium, for which he had purchased another ticket.

He had practiced firing grenades with the M-79

for many hours in a Mexican desert area and was very accurate.

In his mind, Miguel's plan was effective, simple, and foolproof. He also decided that, if he missed, he would just make a new plan and try again.

For a routine hit, the assassin would normally rig a beat-up old car with explosives and park it next to his intended victim's car and then detonate the mobile bomb by remote control when his target moved to his car. To him, this was just another hit, a little more complicated than most, but for more money. He had no loyalty to country, anything, or anybody. His loyalties changed constantly to suit himself.

The killer's final preparation had been to walk around Cleveland in drag for a few nights to see if anybody could tell he was a man. The experience excited him, acting like he was a woman, and this made him upset and angry with himself. The deadly killer would view himself in the mirror, dressed in drag, and rub his hands up and down his nylons, getting even more aroused. Afterward, he would become very angry with himself and become more psyched for the planned killing. His disguise had been successful and had even attracted a few whistles and stares from male passersby. This also secretly aroused Miguel and made him even more angry and ready to kill.

At Cleveland Stadium, dressed in a large fur-collared coat, fancy boots, dress, and fur hat, Miguel watched the introduction of the President of the United States and the two teams. Just beyond the stadium rippled the surface of Lake Erie while the stars and stripes waved within during the playing of the National Anthem. The stone-cold killer was unaffected. He simply watched and waited as the game began.

Miguel was thorough. He had never been suspected of his crimes. Everything was carefully planned ahead of time, each detail meticulously thought out. That was why something was bothering him. He didn't know what.

His eyes kept straying to number eighty for the Denver Broncos. The man was about six feet four and was white but had a very dark complexion. He also kept looking up into the stands. The Broncos' coach, Dan Reeves, signaled number eighty over and sent him out to the huddle with a play. The quarterback, John Elway, was noted for putting tiny cross-shaped bruises on receivers' chests from the imprint of the football's seams after his bullet passes. He ran a play-action pass and threw one of those bullets to number eighty, who caught it while instantaneously getting sandwiched by vicious hits from the strong safety and right cornerback from Cleveland.

As he got up and walked back to the huddle, the announcer declared that number eighty was Mark Jackson and was one of the Broncos' noted receivers referred to as the "Three Amigos." Jackson still kept looking up into the stands, but the assassin finally relaxed when he concluded that the Broncos' wide receiver must have been looking for a friend or relative in the audience.

As John Elway marched the Denver team down the field, the Browns' fans started going crazy trying to cheer their team on. They were jumping and screaming in the stands, and Atencio saw his opportunity to blow up the leader of the free world. His hand slipped under the thick coat and grabbed the stock of the deadly grenade launcher.

Then something on the field caught his eye. Mark Jackson had removed his helmet and was staring at him while reaching into the top of a Gatorade ice cooler. Something was very familiar about him. Something that instantly alarmed Miguel.

The wide receiver pulled out a folding-stock carbine with a laser scope mounted on top and quickly tore it from its protective plastic bag. All of a sudden, it hit Miguel: He had seen a feature about the Broncos' Three Amigos. Mark Jackson, Ricky Nattiel, and Vance Johnson were all black and all three were relatively short. The imposter wearing number eighty was white with a very dark complexion and powder-blue eyes that could even be seen up into the stands. He also stood six feet four and Miguel remembered that Mark Jackson was the shortest of the Three Amigos, standing five feet nine at the most.

Quickly, the assassin pulled the rear sight up on the M-79, then he saw the phony receiver wave his right arm three times, and all the lights in the stadium suddenly went out.

The last thing Miguel Atencio saw was the little red lazer light from the gun as it centered between his eyes. There was a muzzle flash, and the back of his head splattered blood and brain matter over three rows of spectators behind him.

The crowd was screaming as the stadium lights came back on. A number of fans in the general area of the assassin pulled weapons and Secret Service ID's out of their coats and converged on the dead killer's body. The imposter player, carbine in hand, scrambled up into the stands. In the meantime, Secret Service agents spirited away the President.

Seeing that Miguel was indeed beyond repair, the fake number eighty bent over and picked up a miniature US flag a fan had dropped and stuck it into the bullet hole in Miguel's forehead.

He said, "That was for Fancy and the United States, you son of a bitch."

The man looked down at the dead killer's body and remembered the last time he had seen him. He had just finished making love with the only woman he had ever loved, a CIA operative named Fancy Bird. After rescuing her from a prison in Libya, he and she were close to escaping the clutches of Wacky Qadhafi in Tripoli. They had made love on a boat in the harbor at Tripoli. He'd walked up the steps of the boat they were on only to turn and see the woman he loved take a bullet right between the eyes. The bullet had been fired by Miguel Atencio. He had rammed into Atencio with a tackle and knocked him overboard, but fire from Libyan police and soldiers who had surrounded the boat drove him back. He barely escaped Libya with his own life but had vowed that someday he and Atencio would meet again and he would kill him. He had just attained that goal.

He then returned to the field and received a high five from the real Mark Jackson and other players and coaches and ran off the field to the cheers of the fans.

The President of the United States, Secret Service agents, and several diplomats and advisors sat in the conference room of a national guard armory in downtown Cleveland as the tall good-looking fake Bronco walked in. Everybody in the room, including the President, stood and applauded him. He walked up to the President, they shook hands, and the President handed him a cup of coffee.

"Thank you, Major Tracker," the President said enthusiastically. "You saved my life. I still can't figure out how you spotted him as the hit man."

The tall handsome man removed his jersey and shoulder pads revealing well-defined, powerful muscles and a washboard stomach.

He pulled the orange jersey back on and said, "It really wasn't that difficult, Mr. President. After US intelligence got the hot tip about the assassination attempt, the Secret Service manned every ticket booth with hidden video cameras. We figured that the hit man would buy tickets for two different seats, as it would be the only safe way to hide after killing you. Most of those who came back to buy extra tickets always asked for seats adjoining or near the ones they already had.

There were just a few exceptions, so I was assigned to watch the people in those seats."

"Yes, but how did you identify this Atencio character since he was dressed like a woman?" the President asked.

Tracker responded, "Well, sir, as you probably know, I can push on my right eyebrow, and my vision will zoom in with a telephoto view, and then by pushing on the sensor implanted under my left eyebrow, I can zoom back to normal eyesight. I kept zooming in on each one of the target suspects and finally noticed that the hit man, Miguel Atencio, had an Adam's apple."

The President was puzzled. "I still don't understand."

Tracker continued, "Well, Mr. President, only men have Adam's apples; women don't."

"I'll be damned," the President replied. "Wasn't he the man who killed your girlfriend in Libya last year?"

Tracker cleared his throat, a sad look on his handsome face. "Yes, sir. Yes, he was, and it was only Providence that enabled me to get him. I had vowed that I would."

The President smiled thoughtfully. "Natty, I don't think that there has ever been any doubt in anybody's mind that you would nail him or accomplish anything else you set your mind to."

Nathaniel Hawthorne Tracker had been an All-American wide receiver at the Air Force Academy before starting an outstanding career that began with his becoming a radar officer. Although he trained and competed extensively, acheiving a second-degree black belt in Tae Kwon Do, he still wanted more action, so he attended flight school.

By the time he achieved the rank of major, Natty Tracker was an "ego driver," a pilot of the F-15C Eagle and was considered one of the Sierra Hotel (Shit Hot) pilots in the Air Force. Flying the rugged and narrow corridor over the Bering Sea separating the United States and the USSR, Natty piloted out of Elmendorff Air Force Base at Anchorage, Alaska.

Unfortunately, one night while returning from a karate class, his 1963 split-window Corvette was forced off the road by a drunk driver, and he ended up permanently blind.

After learning to overcome his supposed handicap and being medically discharged from the Air Force, Major Tracker set out to regain his sight. His father, a retired command sergeant major, was one of the Army's first computer experts. Tracker developed the OPTIC and SOD Systems.

Based on simple sonar like a bat's, the Sonar Optic Device sent sonar pulses from special glasses and then received their echoes, translating them into beeps through a special ear plug. The closer the object, the faster the beeps, and the larger the object, the deeper the tone of the beeps. Using this system, he was able to effectively "see" with his ears.

The OPTIC System was an acronym for OPtical Tracking Initiation Contrivance and was a lot more complicated than the SOD System. Working with a team of the nation's top opthamologists and computer experts, Natty developed a set of glasses that had lenses similar to a video camera. These plugged into two fiber optic filaments that protruded through his eyebrows. Each of these was connected to a bio-compatible fiber-optic net attached to the corresponding optic nerve. This system stimulated the optic nerves in whatever patterns the glasses viewed, very similar to the series of dots that comprises a video picture. The SOD System was used in conjunction with this since cameras do not have depth perception.

Prior to that time and following, Natty had developed many inventions, some of which he had sold to the US government, such as the TRACKER System. This was a simple wrist device with a miniaturized infrared sensor that picked up body heat from people and animals and let the wearer know the target's distance, speed, and direction of travel.

Tracker had since greatly improved the OPTIC System. He had another operation in which an improved nerve-stimulating fiber-optic mesh was attached to his optical nerves. NASA optical specialists had developed miniaturized lenses for Natty that were actually soft contact lenses permanently attached to the eyeball connected to fiber-optic filaments extending through his eyeballs. Sensor devices were implanted in the skin under each eyebrow which could be pushed to zoom Natty's eyesight in and out telescopically. His glasses were greatly improved, and he would occasionally wear them to see incredibly long distances in sharp detail, to see at night with daylight clarity, or to see with a limited X-ray capability in certain circumstances.

With the wealth he amassed from the sale of his inventions, Tracker bought a palatial home at the base of Cheyenne Mountain, headquarters for NORAD, America's self-defense brain, at Colorado Springs, Colorado.

Tracker had one grandparent who was a blond-haired, blue-eyed Norweigan, another was black, another was a Tonto Apache, and another who was Assiniboin Sioux. Hence, he grew up with a dark olive complexion, wavy black hair, and striking powder-blue eyes.

Learning from his American Indian relatives, he developed a deep love for wildlife and the outdoors. Starting out with chipmunks and squirrels, he had become a very proficient tracker and made a concerted effort to live up to his family name. By the time he was a teenager, Natty could almost track the day-old flight pattern of a sparrow through an overcast sky.

Working as an independent contractor for the federal government, Natty became the ultimate private detective, tackling ticklish jobs for the US, jobs that could bring embarrassment to the government if he were an actual employee.

The President had assigned a crusty old retired Army general named Wally Rampart to be Natty's contact man in the government. Wally, an Undersecretary of State, reported directly to the President. He also loved Natty Tracker and would go to hell for him.

GREEN LIGHTNING

After Tracker's first mission, the government rewarded him with his own "sterilized" F-15E Eagle with the latest in technology and equipment. He rid the world of a much-wanted terrorist called The Ratel while rescuing an Air Force pilot from a prison in Libya, but not before being tortured and losing his left ring finger in the process. He also left his lover there, Dr. Fancy Bird, when she was executed by the now-deceased mercenary terrorist Miguel Atencio.

Tracker usually didn't waste time or energy worrying about life's negative twists and turns, but in the case of Doctor Bird, he couldn't help himself. Her death hurt him deeply, although she too was a spy, and they both understood the rules. Tracker had made a vow to himself, and that was to exact revenge on her behalf against Atencio.

Miguel Atencio was a beast whose mother, like the mother of The Ratel, had been a Havana prostitute. Miguel's mother was a heroin addict and had gotten him started on drugs when he was seven years old. He gladly took them to blunt the pain of his life. His mother used to sell his body to pedophiles, so he had suffered severe sexual and physical abuse. Because of the sick and sordid lifestyle he had been brought into and was forced to endure, his adult life became what one would have expected. He was a brutal and sadistic killer and rapist.

His mother was the first victim of his sadistic mentality. Miguel Atencio tortured and murdered her while loaded on PCP, "angel dust." It was done to satisfy a savage curiosity and to prove to himself that he was worthy of the terrorist mindset he had attained. He thought he was a hero by killing for money for various causes, especially if they were anti-American. Miguel became an internationally acclaimed hit man, but now, thanks to Natty Tracker, he was just another dead thug.

Natty wondered what nature of beast he'd have to deal with next.

2.

Please Don't Beat the Daisies

HENRIETTA LYNN JAMES was a very cute five-year-old girl with long curly tresses that looked as if they had been dipped in honey and hung out in summer sunshine with the melting honey ready to run down and drip off of the ends.

"No, Daddy! No, it hurts!" she screamed as her father raped her.

This was not the first time her father had done this to her. As he had in previous vicious assaults, he told her that he loved her so much, he just wanted to be closer to her, and this was how. He also warned her, again, not to ever tell anybody what they had done, because she was just a little girl and nobody would believe her. He also told her that she would be put in jail.

She screamed and cried and turned her head from side to side, as he kept up the act; but then on that day, the tears suddenly stopped. She knew that afterward there would be more words of warning about her being put in jail if anybody found out. She knew that her father would cry and rub her pretty hair and tell her how sorry he was, and how much he loved her, and how it would never happen again, but she knew that it would; it always did.

Her father lay asleep on the couch an hour later, mouth open, with loud snoring coming from his thick neck. She looked at the little scar on her finger from the time she had picked up his razor and touched it. The only thing his own abusive father had left with him, he had always chosen to shave with it instead of either of the electric shavers he had received on his college graduation or the nice Schick he had received upon his graduation from medical school.

Carefully holding the handle just right, Henrietta pulled the blade down and across the exposed throat of Doctor Jeremy Walter James. His eyes immediately opened in horror and stared at the ceiling as blood immediately gurgled in his throat and started pouring out the sides of his mouth.

Sheer panic registered on his face as he sat up and stared in shock at his cute little five-year-old Henrietta, bloody razor in her hand, and it was then that the realization sank in that she had just slit his throat.

Henrietta Lynn James had slit the throat of her father, that beloved obstetrician who had helped so many children and expectant mothers. The man who was past-president of the local chapter of the Lion's Club. The man who had turned breech babies around. The man who had performed Caeserean sections and saved the lives of

GREEN LIGHTNING

babies and mothers alike. The man who gave ten percent of his gross income to the local First Presbyterian Church where he was an elder. The man who had been a vice president of the city's Chamber of Commerce. The man who gave ten turkeys to needy families each Christmas. The man who had taken away the innocence of Henrietta's youth. The man who had taken away her last vestiges of sanity when she was still so young. The man who was supposed to protect her more than anybody else in the world. She had slit the throat of her father, the monster.

It might have been easier on her mentally if he had been a drug addict like Miguel Atencio's mother. And it might have been easier if her father had had beady eyes and had worn a dirty raincoat and tennis shoes. It wasn't easy when he wore tailored suits and looked a lot like Tom Selleck and had been president of his senior class in school. Then again, he was her father, and nothing could have made it easy for her.

She grinned coyly, as if she had just picked her daddy a handful of daisies and was going to surprise him with them. The color of his face was ashen as he tried to speak and couldn't find the strength to stand.

Sweetly, she said, "You'll never do that again, Daddy."

She wiped the blade and handle on his shirt and went immediately to her room to take her daily nap before Mommy came home from work. She knew Mommy would pick up the razor, and she had seen things about fingerprints on television. She also thought the police would believe her if she was brave and acted really frightened when she told them that her mommy had cut Daddy's throat. She would tell them that Mommy saw Daddy with a naked lady doing nasty things. That would fix Mommy, she figured, for not believing her when she kept trying to tell her about all the things Daddy had done to her.

Henrietta, or "Hank" as she had been nicknamed, recalled the incident twenty-three years later, as she flirtingly stared across the rim of her wine glass at the tall handsome lawyer. The attorney was six feet three and strikingly good-looking. An honors graduate of Harvard Law, he was one of those guys who was always picked first. The shape of Hank's legs was the very first thing that captured his eye. They were long, lithe, and very muscular. Hank had, in fact, broken several cross-country records in high school.

Her foster mother never missed a meet, but secretly her foster father had never missed a chance to satisfy his pedophiliac desires by bribing Hank with gifts and money for her sexual favors. By graduation, Hank had only two true friends; one was her foster mother, and the other was her friend and lover Karen Carr. She loved them both so much that she gave them secret gifts.

She seduced her foster father one night with the little sexual games she had learned so well and talked him into letting her skip school the next day. She promised him many exciting things if he would take her out of town to a nice hotel and make love with her all day. He told his wife he had a business trip, and Hank cut school.

When the police found his body the following day in the hotel, his body had been horribly mutilated, and his wallet was gone. They chalked it up to a vicious attack by a hooker and her pimp.

Two weeks later, Karen's father, a salt-and-pepper-haired Free Will Baptist minister, was found with his throat slit, his lifeless body nailed to the large cross above his choir loft. The crotch of his pants had been cut away, but otherwise he had been fully clothed. The police didn't even consider the possibility that both murders had been committed by the same perpetrator.

Both of these killings remained locked in Hank's mind, as did all the other killings; but as with the others, they were her secret gifts to the women she loved. She knew she couldn't let the women know about her gifts to them, but knowing that she had done it made her feel good. Hank felt she was almost Godlike in her ability to snuff out the lives of those who surrounded and who could potentially bring harm to her loved ones.

For several years now, she had been keeping a collection of trophies from each of those she had killed stored in jars of formaldehyde and neatly arranged in symmetrical rows on the built-in bookcase in her west wing guest room. Her wealthy foster mother felt that the sun rose and set on Hank, so she had left her with a mansion and a tidy fortune.

Hank never had to work, but she chose to and

did so around books, because she loved to read. As a matter of fact, all she did was read or go hunting. She would sometimes go into the guest room and sit in a large over-stuffed armchair and stare at the assorted "trophies" and recall the memories of obtaining each one. Some were large and some were small, some were black but most were white, some were circumcised and a few were not. Hank was very proud of her collection, though, because they were hers. She had collected them with her own wits and wiles. She would sit and stare at her prized possessions while she reveled in the memory of the terror on the face of each of the hunted when she'd collected her trophy.

Each of those hunted who gave up a trophy to her then became a member of her "gallery." The gallery sat in her mind and cheered her on each time she collected a new trophy. Sometimes they cheered and clapped and whistled while she was flirting with another victim, because they knew the methods she was employing would work on any of the hunted. They had been encouraging her to get more inventive, too.

A number of law enforcement agencies had extensive files on Hank, this ferocious new serial killer. Being chauvinists, many of them figured the serial killer was a homosexual man because of the sexual disfigurement involved and the sheer horror of the attacks. Most female serial killers had been, to date, nurses who poisoned patients, nursing home attendants who drugged or smothered elderly patients, and other less vi-

GREEN LIGHTNING

olent killers. Male serial killers, on the other hand, were usually more violent in their methods and often included torture and sexual abuse of their victims. Hank, as feminine and beautiful as she seemed, was probably the most dangerous and ferocious serial killer of all time because of her methods of seduction and then death and mutilation of her victims. It was certainly easy to understand how she could have become such a killer, but nobody cared now. They just wanted it to stop. Many hard-core cops had secretly experienced chills and outright terror when they arrived at the crime scene after Hank had taken a trophy.

Her best hunting adventure was to get her victim into a position where she could bite the trophy off and then kill him while he screamed in agony. This time she was going to try for a "bite-off trophy," and then shoot the man while he screamed. Hank had never shot any of the hunted. Most she slashed or stabbed, one died of a heart attack, one she poisoned, and another she had run over. When Hank had taped her new weapon to the inside of her thigh, she knew it would probably tear her skin away when she pulled the snub-nosed Smith and Wesson Model Ten out, but she figured seeing the .38 caliber go off into her prey would make it more fulfilling. She was excited about her new hunting technique and pictured grinning up into the face of the handsome attorney with her trophy in her mouth and then shooting him right under his chin.

Alice, her coworker at the library, acted like she

had been in love with him, but Hank knew she could use her hunting techniques to make him desire her. She liked Alice, so she had decided to give her a silent gift. Alice would never have her heart broken by this man who would inevitably violate her and destroy her trust, as all men eventually did. Hank had decreed that Alice was too good a woman to be made to suffer so.

The lawyer stared across the table at the cleavage of the well-endowed beauty with the waist-length golden hair. Her green eyes had been hinting of secret pleasures all night long, and he wanted to hunt for those treasures. The man had loved Alice, but he couldn't help himself when this gorgeous creature started flirting with him earlier in the afternoon at the courthouse. He daydreamed about those long tanned legs being wrapped around his waist. He tried to picture the large firm breasts without cover, the flat stomach and firm buttocks. Now, his heart skipped a beat as she grinned impishly and leaned across the table, and then he felt her hand as it seized and caressed his erection under the tablecloth. Embarrassed, he looked around the Italian restaurant, but nobody was looking.

Trying to be debonair, he caught his breath and said softly, "Would you like that?"

She grinned and said, "Of course; I like to collect them, you know."

She gave a little chuckle, and he, at first taken aback by her strange statement, joined her, and soon they were both laughing loud enough that several other diners turned to look at them. Arm

GREEN LIGHTNING

in arm, they walked out of the busy restaurant giggling and staring deep into each other's eyes.

The Harvard man felt he had never seen a woman so sensual, so sexy, or one he wanted so much, and he could hardly breathe knowing that he would have her very shortly.

In her brain, the gallery was clapping and cheering loudly. She had asked to go out into the country and "park," like teenagers, on an old wooded road. The way she said "park" and the way he had parked as a teeny-bopper were two completely different things. She was young, fresh, and exciting, but she was not innocent.

He decided right then that, if she liked to collect penises, she was definitely going to add his to her collection. Little did he know Hank had decided the matter long before she had started the hunt that day.

Alice was away from the library for a long time after the funeral, but Hank knew it was for the best. She felt Alice would have actually thanked her had she known that eventually her fiance would betray her and violate her. Again, she felt as if she had done a Godly deed and removed another man from this world. He was now a member of the gallery. And he held the special distinction of joining the gallery with a bullet. He was the first one, but not the last, Hank decided. She did want to get a more powerful gun, though, since she felt it would be more glorious if she could see more damage when sending a hunted to the gallery.

The one incredible coincidence Hank couldn't have known was what happened on the fateful night she shot the lawyer. She did not know that she had been followed when she and the young attorney had been out on the date. She did not know that when she was with the young attorney on the hood of the car on the deserted country road, there were two pairs of eyes observing them both. Hank was not aware that at the moment of complete ecstacy when she bit down and then fired her pistol up under his chin, that two watchers witnessed the entire scene, silently applauding her from afar.

Mr. All-American, it seems, had actually worked his way through Harvard selling computer codes from his father's New York stock brokerage firm to a Japanese student. He had then convinced several other students to sneak computer codes from their families' businesses, and he had made money acting as a broker for them and the Japanese student who had paid him quite handsomely. He had been quite successful, as his family was New England "old money," and there had been no shortage of young men looking for an easy way to increase the family fortune.

The Japanese student continued to maintain contact with the attorney, who by that time, was selling business secrets of some of his more lucrative clients to the Oriental. He had grown to the point in the business that he had finally started guessing things about the Japanese man, such as who he was working for and why.

The two pairs of eyes that had been watching

Hank and the lawyer belonged to two hit men hired by the Japanese gardener at the lawyer's mansion. They were paid well and were ordered to kill him. Both figured the gardener must have been having an affair with the target's wife. The hit men gave the photographs of Hank and the young lawyer to his gardener along with their full report. Knowing that no investigator would look for the two thugs, he shot them both and buried them in the garden.

Two months later the gardener quietly quit his job and boarded a plane for Tokyo, having told his new employers that he was returning to his homeland in Okinawa to take over his uncle's fishing business, a complete fabrication.

The mild little gardener was soon trying to secure a civilian job at the US Army Seventh Field Hospital in Camp Oji in Tokyo. He wanted to get a job as an air-conditioning maintenance man so he could try to get access to the Army's computers in the massive hospital complex.

PACCOM, the Pacific Command, was one of the few major military headquarters that the RRK had, to date, not penetrated effectively. They were learning more about Hank at that time, and were developing plans to use her in the near future.

3.

The Jackal of the Cloth

REVEREND CLYDE KAROL Ormand was the pastor of the Grace Holy Brethren Freewill Evangelical Church of Spartanburg, South Carolina. He had brains that seemed to have been in a demolition derby for food processors due to his five-hundred-dollar-a-day cocaine habit that had started with a few seemingly innocent lines snorted at parties in Bible College. To support his rather expensive habit, besides selling the Word of God, Brother Ormand had taken to peddling nose candy to some of the less savory citizens of Spartanburg as well as some of his more prominent parishioners.

His voracious consumption of the white powder had long since eliminated the last vestiges of spirituality he had brought into his study of the Word. In fact, he had been spending most of his time at home thinking about a recent tryst in the baptismal with an amply endowed fifteen-year-old girl. They laughed and giggled and snorted coke and sated each other's sexual appetites with the innocent laughter and gaiety of two children playing in the bathtub.

Earlier that day, Pastor Ormand had gotten into a red-faced, vein-bulging argument with a youth minister from a local Methodist church. The younger preacher had remarked about his respect and admiration for the famous television minister and author Doctor Robert Schuller. The Reverend Brother Ormand referred to Doctor Schuller as a secular humanist and said that the TV minister was an "adequate philosopher" with his "power of possibility" thinking and his so-called "Be-Happy Attitudes," but he was definitely not preaching the literal Holy Word as it was written in the Scriptures.

The youth minister calmly stated that Doctor Schuller had always preached a message of love, dignity, and self-respect, and that was indeed the overall message of the Bible. Indignant and enraged, the charismatic doper unconsciously felt his carefully combed and sprayed pompadour hairdo to insure his anger hadn't popped a strand out of place and then slammed his neatly manicured hand down on his worn, ever-present Bible.

Gritting his teeth in an effort to control his rage, Clyde said, "Brother, this is the Holy Word of God, and I only preach the literal Word of the Lord as it is written in these Holy Scriptures. There is one way and one way only to enter the portals of Heaven, my friend, and that is through a personal belief that Christ is your heavenly savior and died on the cross for your sins and ascended into Heaven. Once you have received Him as your personal savior, you should then be baptized in the Holy Spirit. You and Doctor Schuller and everybody else that promotes materialistic endeavors and not the literal interpretation of His Holy Word are in danger of eternal damnation. More importantly, you must preach the opportunity for complete and eternal salvation through a firm and public affirmation of Jesus Christ as one's personal savior."

The whole experience with the young Methodist minister was quite traumatic and unsettling for Brother Ormand. In fact, he was so unnerved by the incident that he had to retire immediately to his church office and chill out with a Quālude or two.

Clyde Ormand had been a good boy while growing up. The son of a Southern Baptist minister, he had wanted to be a preacher or missionary ever since first grade. Like many preachers' kids, he did, however, try to prove that he wasn't a goody-two-shoes with his peers in high school and college. Unfortunately, he had an addictive personality, and it didn't take much for him to get hooked on cocaine. As the addiction progressed, he fell deeper and deeper into a spiritual vacuum.

The money, highs, and glamour were not more attractive to him than an afterlife, but he didn't hesitate to sell the afterlife to buy more highs. He had learned to become a God-salesman when he really believed in what he was doing. Clyde found he could sell the message and that people believed in what he said. After becoming a cokehead, he simply preached what he had practiced for so many years, and the crowds, for the most part, believed that the forty-year-old minister was sincere.

Pastor Ormand received his shipments of coke from an air cargo pilot who would pick up corpses in Columbia and deliver them to the United States. The corpses were actually purchased from a mortician owned by one of the many drug cartels. He would surgically remove the thigh bones of the dead person and replace them with scented and hermetically sealed plastic tubes containing cocaine. The bodies were then delivered to Reverend Ormand's funeral home which he had inherited from his father.

His older brother had inherited their father's thriving slaughterhouse, so having been introduced into the world of "warm snow" by his brother Clyde, he helped dispose of the bodies at night. He and Clyde carried them into the slaughterhouse after removing the coke and ground them into hamburger along with beef products and distributed the end product to grocery stores throughout the southeastern United States.

One day the bodies stopped arriving. Not long after, Brother Clyde learned of the untimely demise of the South American mortician. Paranoid, he bit his nails and waited, and waited.

After a month, the church secretary escorted a Japanese gentleman into his office who said he was a missionary from their international church headquarters.

Once alone, the supposed missionary reached

into his worn, hollowed-out Bible and retrieved a plastic bag of white powder, which he tossed in front of the pastor's startled face.

"From now on, Reverend," the Japanese man said, "you will deal with me for your coke."

Clyde gulped and said, "Okay, what will this cost?"

"No money," the man said, smiling. "We just want you to visit your church headquarters occasionally. Find out what type of computer the church uses, where they bank, what their access codes are. That's all."

"Who are you?" Reverend Ormand asked.

"You don't care. Just do as I ask with no questions, and we will give you the same amount of cocaine you were receiving before," the man said.

"What if I don't want to? What if I want to just get straight?" Clyde asked.

The well-dressed Oriental smiled and walked over to the Reverend's television set and turned it on. It was mounted high on the wall amid volumes of theological esoterica. Next to it sat a VCR with which the good preacher could watch his previous week's captivating sermon while getting loaded on high-grade blow. The television was also connected to the local cable service.

The Japanese man handed the remote to the preacher and asked, "What is your favorite cable station?"

The preacher thought a second and replied, "The Disney Channel."

The man pulled a leather case out of his suit pocket and extracted a pocket computer. He pulled an antenna out of the computer and punched in some numbers. He watched the miniature screen for a second and smiled when a tiny beep sounded. He put the computer back into the leather case and returned it to his pocket.

He smiled at the man of the cloth and said, "Please turn your TV set to the Disney Channel."

Clyde did so and stared at the screen, eyes transfixed in horror, as he saw the burned face of the Columbian mortician. The man was screaming and had two very large Japanese strongmen holding him by the arms and hair. His eyebrows, moustache, and part of his hair looked to have been burned off by cigarettes or cigars.

One of the burly men, who appeared to be a Sumo wrestler, smiled toward the camera and held a piano wire with wooden handles on each end in a loop over the mortician's head. He slipped the garrotte over the man's head and tightened it around the screaming throat. Pulling the handles, the brute spun and lifted the man onto his back and pulled forward on the handles. The thin wire sliced neatly through the neck, between two vertebrae, and the head popped off cleanly and dropped onto the floor with a dull thud. The cameraman zoomed to the sightless, bulging eyes. Clyde Ormand fell into his chair with an anxiety attack. He vomited into his wastebasket.

The Japanese man smiled politely and said, "Pastor Ormand, would you please help us in our endeavors?"

Totally shaken, Clyde just shook his head affirmatively as the Japanese man walked to the office door.

With a raspy voice, Clyde asked, "What should I call you?"

The man thought, smiled again, and said, "Sir."

4.

Home Sweet Home

TRACKER OPENED HIS eyes, looked out the bedroom window, and saw the Will Rogers Memorial in the distance. Located at the end of a ridgeline of Cheyenne Mountain, it looked out over the city of Colorado Springs sprawled at the prairie's edge at the base of the majestic Pike's Peak. Natty turned on his side and looked into the almond-shaped eyes of the thirty-year-old Native American beauty lying across his muscular chest. Her black hair fell off her shoulders and slid across her ample copper breasts. Natty smiled and pushed it gently back behind her shoulders. He kissed her softly on the nose as she smiled.

He got out of bed and said, "How would you like a nice breakfast in bed?"

She reached over and picked up an eagle feather from the nightstand. The beautiful Missy Antelope, of the Oglala Sioux, gave Natty a smoldering look and smile. She replied, "I'd much rather have you get back under the covers and show me some more of those magical things you can do with feathers."

He laughed and patted her on the butt. She giggled as he walked out of the room and into the long upstairs hallway. Wearing only bikini briefs, he stopped near the head of the wide, winding stairway, jumped up, and grabbed the overhead chinning bar and did fifty chin-ups without cheating. He felt her eyes boring into his massive back and grinned to himself as he heard her sneak back into bed. He wouldn't let her know he knew she was watching him perform this daily ritual.

Tracker went down to the kitchen to prepare a sumptuous breakfast of eggs benedict, pink grapefruit, sweet rolls, and coffee. He carried both meals up to his lover on a silver tray with a bud vase in the center with a single pink rose.

Natty had met Missy two months earlier at a tribal pow wow in South Dakota. She was a kindergarden teacher and had a very special way with children. She also had a very special way with Natty Tracker.

They enjoyed the tasty breakfast, and Missy, still nude, picked up the fragrant pink rose and smelled it. Natty, in the meantime, picked up the eagle feather and waved it in front of her.

"Like feathers, huh?" he asked.

She grinned impishly and replied, "I'm tickled pink."

They made long, slow, passionate love for several hours and fell asleep in each other's arms. While they slept, Tracker's subconscious mind automatically catalogued different sounds: a dis-

GREEN LIGHTNING 37

tant clicking noise was identified as an incoming FAX in his oak-paneled computer room; a low hum was the air conditioner kicking on; another hum outside was the automatic skimmer for the pool and jacuzzi. A barely audible click made Natty's eyes pop open.

His mind tried to register the noise. It was coming from the game room directly below his bedroom. He heard another click. His mind knew the noise and rapidly fast-forwarded through old files. It hit him instantly: the sound was that of the black cover of an M-60 machine gun being snapped into place over a belt of ammunition. Tracker grabbed Missy, along with the bud vase, rolled off of the bed with her, and dragged her into the bathroom as 7.62 millimeter bullets tore through the floor and Natty's king-size bed in a deafening, explosive staccato.

Natty jumped on top of the toilet tank with his feet in the bowl and held Missy tightly on his lap as the bullets walked into his bathroom and tore through the floor. They stopped, and he jumped out of the commode and quickly lay Missy in the bathtub, signaling her to keep quiet.

Natty, hearing footsteps running into the bedroom, broke the neck of the bud vase and dived straight through the bathroom door, his left hand in front and the right with the jagged vase following. His left hand grabbed the stock of a MAC-11 machine pistol, his right hand drove the jagged glass into the abdomen of a black-garbed ninja. The man screamed as the deadly automatic pistol went off, peppering the walls with .45 caliber bullet holes.

Natty let go of the bud vase and jerked the barrel of the weapon upward and watched the spouting flames send the ninja's face into the ceiling in a human volcano of blood and flesh. He ripped it loose from the assailant's hands and dived over the end of his bed as a second ninja assassin ran in his door firing another MAC-11. Tracker fired at the man while somersaulting onto the floor, and the bullets hit the other's weapon, tearing it from his hands.

Natty's weapon ran out of ammunition. The ninja pulled off his mask and grinned at Natty as he pulled a shuriken, a six-pointed throwing star, from his black sleeve. The killer was Japanese. Tracker stood totally naked, facing the ninja, knowing that the deadly steel blades of the shuriken had been dipped in a neurotoxic poison that would kill him within seconds. Natty also knew that the killer could throw the small multi-bladed knife with pinpoint accuracy.

Tracker reached up, and acting like he was scratching it, he pushed on his left eyebrow, and his eyes zoomed into an extreme close-up of the killer's pupils. From his many years of martial arts training, Natty knew that the pupil dilates very slightly each time a new thought enters one's mind. This would give the ninja a one-quarter-second slower reaction time, and that was all Tracker needed. The pupil flared, and Natty threw the empty machine pistol at the man's eye as he dived forward in a somersault, pushing his eyebrow on the way. The star sailed over his head and stuck into the wall, and the assassin ducked the gun.

In the meantime, Tracker had rolled over and his foot lashed out, the blade catching the killer on the kneecap, breaking the leg. Still rolling up to his feet, he lunge-punched the man on the point of the chin, shattering it and breaking the hinge joints of the jaw.

Natty grabbed two loaded magazines out of the unconscious man's black clothing and loaded the two MAC-11s. He ran into the bathroom and handed one of them to Missy after cocking it.

"If anybody comes in the door, just point at their chest and pull the trigger," he hissed.

Very frightened, she nodded, eyes open wide and held it up. He smiled and kissed her on the forehead then ran out the door and into the hallway.

The machine-gunner was waiting for the movement and fired the M-60 through the floor of the balcony from below. Wood splinters flew up into Tracker's exposed legs and bare feet. Quickly slinging the MAC-11 over his shoulder, he jumped, grabbed the chinning bar, and hauled himself up. Looking above him, Natty saw that the skylight was open. He decided to pull himself up and out onto the roof, jump down, and shoot the machine-gunner through the window. Tracker leaped, grabbed the sill, and heard a laugh at the top of the stairs. Another Japanese killer, dressed like a ninja, pointed the M-60 at him. He too, had removed his black hood.

With a low voice the man said, "One hand, Tracker. Hang. One hand, slow, drop gun."

Natty held with his right hand, reached up with his left, and removed the MAC-11 and let it drop to the floor. The Japanese assassin aimed the M-60 at Tracker's sweating chest.

Natty said, "Can I ask you a question?"

"Ask," came the guttural reply.

Natty said, "Why do so many assholes like yourself dress up like old-time ninjas, when you're nothing but thugs and punks? Been watching too many chop-socky movies, huh?"

The killer's face got red, and he stepped up closer to the naked American still hanging from the skylight.

He hissed, "Now you die, funny man."

Natty started urinating on the man's face. He dropped as the assassin gasped and wiped at his face. Tracker executed a side-kick as he was falling and did a judo breakfall as he hit the floor hard. The would-be killer flew backward over the balcony railing, the machinegun going off in a giant arc, and landed face down on the hallway floor below.

Natty grabbed the MAC-11 off the floor along with the ninja's mask, set the mask on the bannister, and slid down the winding staircase, firing at the moaning assassin below. The man died and Natty hit the bottom at a run.

Tracker ran outside and looked around but he saw no one. He turned to reenter the house and dropped quickly, spinning at the sound of a high caliber rifle going off. He brought his weapon up,

GREEN LIGHTNING 41

then saw another ninja, apparently an outside guard, fall out of a tree near his gate. In the distance he saw his neighbor, a KGB spy named Yuri, with a scoped rifle in his hands. The two grinned at each other and Natty gave a wave of gratitude. Yuri waved it off and walked into his house. Yuri, along with several other KGB spies who shared the house with him, had been assigned to keep Tracker under surveillance. Natty knew who they were from the very beginning, and it had become a standing joke between him and Yuri that Tracker would have Domino's pizzas delivered to the Russian agents while they were spying on him. He and Yuri had spoken several times and enjoyed mutual respect.

He checked the rest of the house quickly and returned to the bedroom, hearing approaching sirens in the distance.

Natty revived the unconscious killer upstairs and tried to question him before the police arrived. Missy, wrapped in a robe, sat behind him on the bed and shook.

"Who sent you?" Natty asked.

The killer scratched his head and a pill appeared in his hand. Before Natty could react, the assassin threw the pill into his mouth and bit down on it and swallowed. His body convulsed twice and he died.

Missy screamed and Natty walked over and held her as she started to cry.

"Cyanide capsule," he said softly.

Natty got up, put on some clothes and started searching around the house. He stopped at a control panel by the door and pushed a button that opened the large wrought-iron gate. Several police cars roared in and up the winding driveway, screeching to a halt in front of Natty. He quickly told them what happened, and they swarmed all over his property.

Natty went inside with two cops and walked upstairs to examine the open skylight. He climbed up and out onto the roof and helped one cop up also. On the roof, they discovered three black parachutes and three hammocks attached to hooks at the peak of the roof. Tracker concluded that the three must have skydived onto the roof during the night while he and Missy were out dancing. They then remained on the roof on the slope away from the neighbors' view in the hammocks until daytime. Tracker figured they had opened the skylight before he got home and decided to wait until daylight, figuring his senses would be more alert to unusual noises during the nighttime. He had been rebuilding the mansion for two years, and the one weak area in his security and his alarm system had been his roof. Natty wondered how they knew that. He also wondered who they were and why he had been attacked.

Natty went to his computer room and sent a FAX to Wally Rampart and then he and Missy answered questions from the police.

Missy was shaken up by the incident. Over lunch, she explained that she thought she was in love with Tracker, but his lifestyle was just too frightening for her. She started crying, but smiling warmly, Natty held her and kissed her tears away.

A team from the top secret counter-terrorist Delta Force at Fort Bragg, North Carolina, arrived at nearby Petersen Air Force Base that evening and stayed at Natty's house. They secured the grounds and investigated the break-in while Natty flew Missy home to North Dakota in his Lear jet, one of four aircraft he owned.

The next morning, over breakfast, they all sat around Natty's huge oak table and tried to figure out who the assassins were, and if they had any connection to Atencio's assassination attempt on the President. Tracker wanted to now how they knew that his alarm system was not connected to his roof. There were many questions but no answers.

The following afternoon Tracker was summoned to the coroner's office at the morgue. He was accompanied by the CO of the Delta Team staying with him and Wally Rampart who had flown in during the night. They were met there by the detective from the Colorado Springs police force who was in charge of the investigation.

Introductions were made all around and then the detective said, "Mr. Tracker, I thought you'd be interested in something the coroner's assistant discovered. Doctor?"

The coroner pulled back the three sheets covering the Japanese killers and parted their hair above the right ear. Natty and the others leaned over and looked at a green tattoo of a lightning bolt on the side of the head of each corpse.

At the White House a top secret file was labeled "Green Lightning Investigation."

5.

A Poison Lotus Blossom

DOCTOR JAKI KURIKAWA wore a red silk flowered dress that clung to her curves like spray paint as she walked into the large teak-paneled boardroom. The skyscraper had been built on top of humongous hard rubber shock absorbers so no Tokyo earthquake could do damage to it. Doctor Kurikawa sat down with her back to the tinted windows. The Tokyo shopping crowds and traffic were so far below they could not be heard. Twelve pairs of eyes around the table bored into her as she looked around.

A very distinguished looking salt-and-pepper-haired businessman, Yoshihisa Shibuya, stood up at the head of the table. He walked down the opposite side of the table from Jaki and stopped behind another middle-aged Japanese businessman in a thousand-dollar blue silk suit. The leader put his hands down on the blue-suited gentleman's shoulders.

The leader said, "Doctor Kurikawa, are you

prepared to serve the Ryoku Rai Kyookai with your life if necessary?"

Lowering her eyes, the oriental beauty responded, "Hai."

The leader continued, "To start with, Doctor, Mr. Mishune here invested fifty million dollars of some funds he was entrusted with in an enterprise in France and was stupid enough to think that we would not catch him. He betrayed the Ryoku Rai Kyookai. What you think about that?"

The blue-suited man squirmed as she reached up to her shiny black hair with a sexy smile on her face. She reached into the bun of her hair and grabbed what appeared to be the handle of a chop stick sticking out, and her arm whipped forward. The thin knife shot forward, and with a whoosh, stuck into the man's left eye. His other eye rolled up in his head, and he fell forward on the conference table. The leader grinned as he returned to his seat. Once there, he pushed a button on a control panel in front of him, and two huge brutes came in to remove the body. A third man cleaned the bloodstains.

The leader said, "Very good, Doctor. Eet ees important for all to know that the Ryoku Rai Kyookai shall not be betrayed. Do you understand your assignment?"

Again the beauty responded, "Hai."

He continued, "Thees ees a dangerous assignment, but we have done a lot of research on Miss James. Can you handle it?"

Again, she replied, "Hai," and added, "I know that she is a psychotic killer, but I am a psychiatrist, and I am certain that she will only kill men. I have only to discover the roots of her hatred and turn her menace toward Nathaniel Tracker."

"Are you prepared to do whatever is required to endear yourself to her?" he asked.

"Hai," she responded again, "my family was very poor and because of the Ryoku Rai Kyookai, they are all very wealthy, and I am a psychiatrist."

He smiled warmly, "Your father has always served me well and is completely loyal. Go, but do not fail, or you will die also."

She smiled, "I will not fail. Tracker will die."

Hank sat behind the tall counter in the public library brushing her long beautiful tresses while reading a new release about Vietnam's Montagnards titled *Crossbow*.

"Your hair is very beautiful."

Hank looked up into the beautiful slanted eyes of Jaki Kurikawa who was smiling at the golden-haired killer.

"Thank you," Hank responded warmly. "I see your hair is very long also and it looks beautiful, too. It's hard to tell with it in a bun. How long is it?"

Jaki pulled out the two fake chopsticks stuck through her hair bun and shook it loose; it fell to the top of her buttocks. It was very silky, shiny, and jet black. She wore a skin-tight green silk dress with colorful peacocks embroidered on it, front and back. The two chopsticks were actually thin throwing daggers, with the blades hidden in the bottom of the sticks and released by a slight twist of the thick ends.

Thinking of her professional demeanor, Hank said, "Well, what may I help you with, miss?"

"Oh," Jaki said, "I just love to read and thought I would look at your lovely library. I am brand new in town and this is one of the first places I wanted to visit."

"Oh, I love to read, too," Hank said. "Do you have relatives here, a boyfriend?"

Jaki made a face, "*Please*, I've had enough of men lately . . . too much. I don't know anybody here. I just wanted a fresh start in a new location."

Hank's heart started pounding in her chest, and she wondered if the beautiful Oriental with the mysterious eyes could hear it. She felt a flush come over her body.

The gallery started to yell in her mind, *"Don't tell! Don't tell!"*

She heard her voice speaking, "I would love to be your friend. My name is Henrietta Lynn James, but my nickname is Hank."

Jaki flitted her eyes flirtingly and said, "Oh, that is so kind of you. My name is Jaki Fujioto. Have you had lunch?"

Hank blushed deeply, "No, and it's my lunch hour right now. Come on, it's my treat. What kind of work do you do?"

Jaki said, "I studied psychology a little in college, and I have worked as a rape crisis intervention counselor."

GREEN LIGHTNING 49

The two gorgeous women walked out the door together.

Hank responded, "That must really be rewarding work."

Jaki smiled coyly, "Yes, it really is, but it can be very heartbreaking, too."

Hank said cheerfully, "You and I are so lucky. You know, the way we both look. We don't have to worry about men wanting to hurt us. You know they desire us so much."

Jaki got a hurt look on her face. "Yes, that's what I thought, but I was overpowered and raped."

Hank cheerfully responded, "Where do you want to eat? Hey, why don't we go to my place and I'll fix us a nice lunch?"

"Oh, I don't want to be a bother," Jaki responded.

"No, you won't. It'll be fun. I promise," Hank said enthusiastically. "My car's over there. As a matter of fact, I was going to take the afternoon off. We can get acquainted."

Jaki acted shy. "Well, it sounds like fun. If you're sure?"

Hank beamed, "Of course, I'm sure. I'd love it."

"Okay," the Japanese beauty replied, "let's go."

After a leisurely lunch of salads and club sandwiches, the two took chairs by Hank's olympic-sized pool and had drinks.

Jaki said, "Thank you for lunch; it was delicious, and I can't believe your home. It's just beautiful."

"Thank you," Hank responded. "I inherited it from my mother. Well, my foster mother."

"Were you an orphan?"

"Yes," Hank said convincingly, "both of my parents were killed in a train wreck when I was five years old."

Jaki purposely reached out and touched Hank's hand gently. They looked into each other's eyes.

Jaki spoke softly, "I'm sorry."

Hank cheered up. "Oh, it's okay. I turned out fine."

Jaki flitted her eyebrows. "You certainly did. You're very beautiful."

Hank's heart started pounding in her chest again. She felt her breathing quicken and her ears burned.

Jaki undid the top button on her dress and spoke again, "Phew, that pool looks so inviting today, I wish I would have brought my suit."

Hank blushed again. "Who needs a suit? Nobody can see us here. Let's go swimming."

Jaki grinned, "Okay, I'm game."

Giggling, both women slipped out of their clothing and dived into the pool. The gallery was screaming at Hank in her mind to take Jaki. Jaki was not lesbian, but for the sake of the RRK, she chose to live out her normal homosexual fantasies. She admired Hank's beauty and allowed herself to be aroused by it. Hank was so aroused, she could barely speak.

The two swam around the pool together and then Jaki started a splash fight. The two giggled and splashed each other, magnetically moving

GREEN LIGHTNING

closer and closer. They stopped giggling and stared at each other, both smiling softly. Jaki moved forward and took Hank's cheek in her hands. She slowly moved her face forward and their lips met.

At first they kissed lightly, but then they simultaneously pressed their shapely bodies together and both moaned softly. Hank reached up and took Jaki's breast in her hand and Jaki did the same. They climbed out of the water and made love on a poolside chaise lounge well into the afternoon.

They lay in each other's arms and spoke softly.

Jaki played with Hank's golden tresses and said, "You were just wonderful. I wish I never would have met that man who raped me. I wish I just would have known you."

"Who was he?" Hank asked. "What's his name?"

"His name is Tracker," Jaki responded, "Natty Tracker." Then faking anger, she continued, "I wish somebody would kill the son of a bitch and cut off his dick."

Hank smiled and said, "Now Jaki, you don't mean that."

Tears spilled down her cheeks and Jaki said, "No, I really mean it. I'd give anything if somebody would kill the bastard."

Hank smiled sweetly, "I will."

"What?" Jaki replied, pretending that she was shocked. She was proud of her acting ability.

"I mean it," Hank said calmly. "I'll do it for you. I can, you know."

Jaki pretended to be deep in thought. "You can? Are you sure?"

"Yes, I can," Hank said. "I'll do it for you if you want."

Jaki leaned forward and kissed Hank deeply. They held each other and made love again.

Natty noticed the beautiful blonde and the beautiful Japanese at the corner table as he entered the dining room in the Broadmoor Hotel near his home. They didn't know that he saw them. Hank looked up from her meal as Jaki pointed him out. She was glad, as they had been eating at the Broadmoor for five days watching for him. Pretending that Tracker would be able to recognize her, Jaki had worn a hat and sunglasses as a disguise.

She couldn't have known that Natty was zooming his eyes in on their faces right now as he pushed on his eyebrow. Doing so, Natty could see her eyes through her sunglasses and had already been able to tell that she was Japanese. Because of the recent attack by the ninja-garbed hit men, her nationality made him very suspicious.

The two women thought nothing of it when the tall dark man with the powder-blue eyes put on a pair of tinted glasses when he started to look at his menu. Reaching up as if straightening his glasses, Natty pushed a button on the left frame of his OPTIC System. In the computer room of his palatial mansion, a digital super-VHS tape recorder came on and the monitor showed the picture being recorded. In the foreground was a menu from the Broadmoor, but as Natty pushed a button on the glasses, the picture focus changed, blurring the menu but focusing sharply on two beautiful women seated at a table beyond it. Several beeps sounded as the same image appeared on a large computer monitor. There were several more beeps and the screen read: Picture transmission to INTERPOL; Picture transmission to CIA; Picture transmission to DIA; Picture transmission to Green Lightning file; Picture transmission to White House, Transmissions complete. Standing by: > \

A beep from the improved SOD System in the frame of the glasses let Natty know that his transmission had been completed. When the waiter returned, Natty stood up and let the man know in a voice loud enough for the women to hear that he was going to the restroom. When he returned, they were gone as he guessed they would be. Natty moved over to their table and picked up both of their wine glasses with their napkins and carried them by the stems. He stopped and gave the maitre d' a generous tip and left the restaurant after placing the two stems in separate doggie bags.

Back at his mansion, Natty placed the glasses under a special scanning device that recorded the fingerprints on both glasses and fed them to Washington and INTERPOL. Treated and sterilized sponge-like devices were then used to moisten and remove saliva from the rims of the glasses. These were placed into another computer feeder for analysis through computers in Washington and the National Centers for Disease Control in Atlanta. A smile came to Natty's face a few hours later as he looked over the blood/saliva analyses and saw that neither woman had a sexually-transmitted disease.

Doctor Kurikawa had been born and raised in Tokyo and there was not a lot of information on her, but the file on Henrietta Lynn James was quite thick, as she had been the witness to her mother murdering her father when she was only five. Her mother, according to her file, had been convicted of murder and immediately had a psychotic break, spent one year in a mental institution, and was found dead in her room one day after stabbing herself in the throat with the plastic handle of a toilet bowl scrubber which she had broken off. Henrietta had lived in a number of different foster homes.

Natty sat down at his main computer, tied in to the FBI computer in Washington, and started seeking information. Tracker asked for every killing committed in each city where Henrietta had lived during the period she had resided there. He studied the reports closely and fed every question he could think of that might give him a clue to her personality into the computer.

By the time Tracker was ready to return to the Broadmoor, where he knew Hank would be waiting to "accidentally" meet him, he had a fairly accurate profile worked up on her. He also suspected her of being the serial killer the police were calling, behind closed doors, the "weiner whacker."

He had talked with several very prominent psychiatrists and psychologists about the killings and about her background. They all agreed that if she were indeed the weiner whacker, she had probably been sexually molested as a young girl by her father and then maybe by her foster father too. Natty remembered looking at her in the restaurant and how beautiful she was. This woman was probably the most horrifying serial killer in US history, and Natty found himself feeling sorry for her.

The next evening Natty went to the Broadmoor for dinner. A new Chevrolet followed him, and the video camera shooting through the taillight lens of his new Lamborghini recorded the license number and a punch-in check through his computer center showed it to belong to Thrifty Car Rental in Colorado Springs. Natty smiled as he pulled into the parking lot and got out, zooming his sight in on the driver who had been following him. It was Henrietta Lynn James.

Tracker was seated at a table in the far side of the room, and Hank had herself seated across the dining room from him, not too obvious, but able to make eye contact. She looked up at Natty and he, playing the game like he knew she wanted him to, stared across the room at her with a partial smile on his handsome face. She stared back. In a few minutes a bottle of Cabernet Sauvignon, 1971, was delivered to Hank.

"Compliments of that gentleman across the room," the waiter said.

Hank had him pour a tiny amount in her wine

stem. She swished it around in circles, holding the crystal by the base of the stem. She lifted it to her nose and smelled it, and then swished it around in her mouth and swallowed. She set the glass down and gave the waiter a nod to pour.

With a smile Hank said, "My appreciation to the gentleman. Please ask him if he would like to join me for dinner."

All the while, she maintained seductive eye contact with Tracker, and inside her head, the gallery was jumping up and down and cheering wildly. The waiter relayed the message, and Natty walked over to her table. To other women, watching Natty Tracker crossing the room to their table would have taken away their breaths, but not so with Hank. She simply wondered what his trophy would look like. He sat across from her.

"Hello," he said, "my name is . . ."

Natty stopped speaking as she held her hand up and said, "No. Let's not talk, except with our eyes, like we've been doing."

Natty grinned, and she grinned back. The waiter came and Tracker ordered for her. They both ate their lobster tails in a very sexy suggestive manner. Both, each secretly playing a private game, made love with their eyes. Tracker thought about how easy it must have been for the beauty to seduce and murder scores of men. She was gorgeous. He tried to picture her as a little girl and thought of her father sexually molesting her. It made him sick to his stomach.

He paid the check and left a generous tip. Natty

GREEN LIGHTNING

offered his hand to Hank and helped her out of her chair. They went out to his car but stopped.

Finally speaking, she said, "No, I'll follow."

Natty smiled and escorted her to her rental car, holding the door for her as she climbed in. Hank purposely showed Natty as much thigh as possible as she sat down. His heart did indeed skip a beat as he glanced at her creamy thighs at the top of her smoke-colored nylons, and he saw where they were attached to a lacy black garter belt.

She dropped him at his Lamborghini, and she said briefly, "Nice car."

"Thanks," he said.

Natty helped her out of her car in his big driveway. They kissed long and hard and deeply. Arms around each other's waists, Natty and Hank went into the massive house. Tracker took her immediately upstairs to his bedroom and laid Hank gently on the bed, and he walked over to the door. With a grin and a wink, he locked the massive oak door to his bedroom and flipped the key into the air, caught it, and stuck it in his pocket. Still smiling seductively, she motioned Natty over to the bed.

"I want to feel you inside me," she said with a faked husky voice. "I want to taste you, now."

Natty got a serious look on his face and said, "No, Miss James. I don't want to join the others you've killed and . . . uh . . . decapitated."

She stuck her hand up her dress as if to rub her vagina. An animal howl came from her lips, and her Smith and Wesson Model Ten appeared from between her legs, and she cocked it aiming at

Natty's face. At the same instant his foot swung up in an arc, with an outside crescent kick that struck her wrist, sending the pistol flying across the room. She screamed in pain, and Natty immediately seized her wrists and held her as his closet doors and bathroom door opened to admit a rush of armed men and women. The door unlocked from the outside and more ran in from the hallway. Several attendants seized her and immediately strapped her into a straight-jacket. Snarling like an animal, she tried to bite anybody who came near her. Natty pulled the attendants back and sat on the edge of the bed in front of her.

"I'm sorry for having to trick you. We know about all of the killings and about your father, Miss James. They are going to take you to a hospital and nobody else will hurt you again," he said. "These doctors will help you. I promise."

She looked through Natty with blank eyes and started humming "Mary Had A Little Lamb." He watched her with tears in his eyes as they took her out of the room.

Undersecretary of State Wally Rampart looked like a cross between Teddy Roosevelt, Wilford Brimley, and Winston Churchill, as he paced back and forth in Natty's bedroom, hands behind his back, cigar clenched between his teeth. Tracker grinned.

"There's got be something that can be done to prevent parents from abusing their children, especially sexual abuse," Tracker said.

"There is. It's called a noose. Right now I'm worried about something else, though." Wally growled, "We need to put ya' on ice, Natty. These little black-headed fuckers want to do you in, and we don't know why."

Natty chuckled, "Now, General, don't get so flustered. All we have to do is let them try to kill me, capture a couple, and find out why they're after me."

"Oh bullshit!" Wally roared. "Why don't we hang a fucking target on your ass and let them blow it off with a tank! You dip-brain, Tracker! Fine, fine, Mr. All-American hero; we'll set up a fucking news stand for you in front of the Japanese embassy. No, I've got a better idea," he went on sarcastically. "Why don't you walk up to Mike Tyson and offer him a quarter to give you a shoe shine?"

Tracker started laughing, as did several State Department men and FBI agents in the room.

Natty said, "The first thing we need to do is find Doctor Jaki Kurikawa."

Several men turned and stared as the Japanese beauty walked down Peachtree Street in Atlanta and entered a very large bank. Doctor Kurikawa strolled up to the information desk, bent slightly forward at the waist while she asked a question, and was stared at again by several nearby men. She walked to a small office off the main business area of the bank and was greeted with a handshake by the vice president of the bank at his office door. She was ushered to a seat by him, and he whispered out the door to his secretary, who promptly poured two cups of coffee and took them into the office. He picked up his phone and called the head cashier who picked up a bank draft and headed for his office.

The vice president said, "Mrs. Kyoko, I hope you understand that we must see some identification because of the size of this draft."

"Oh, of course," Jaki replied and opened her purse, producing a phony Georgia driver's license, phony passport, and several credit cards.

The bank executive examined the identification and handed her the bank draft. The money, millions, had been wired from a large bank in Charlotte, North Carolina. The bank had held the funds for the national church headquarters and missionary outreach program of the Grace Holy Brethren Freewill Evangelical Church, the church of the good Reverend Clyde Karol Ormand. Using computers, the Ryoku Rai Kyookai had first consolidated the national funds and the foreign missionary funds of the church into one account in the Charlotte bank. This amount, totalling some twelve million dollars, was then sent to the Atlanta bank via a bank-to-bank wire transfer with simple instructions to give the money to Mrs. Ushi Kyoko, an authorized representative for the church's international mission operating out of Tokyo, Japan. The international mission had set up a phony account in another large Atlanta bank and the bank draft would be deposited into that account. It would again be switched by computer into another account, a phony import/export

GREEN LIGHTNING 61

company, and would ultimately end up in Tokyo in the hands of the RRK.

The RRK had infiltrated many people into bank computer centers all over the world to learn access codes and were transferring funds back to themselves, millions daily, with phony transfers.

Jaki accepted the draft from the head cashier and placed it in her briefcase.

"Can we talk you into depositing your money in our bank?" the vice president asked.

She smiled demurely, "Well, actually our international church board have been discussing a change. They will be meeting again next month on the matter, and you ought to make an appointment to talk with Mr. Jeffrey Albertson (a name she made up on the spot). He'll be back from vacation the first of the month."

"Well, thank you very much," he said as she rose to leave. "I'm very pleased to have met you and wish you Godspeed."

"Why, thank you so much," she said walking out the door, "and may God enrich your life, the way meeting you has enriched mine. Bye."

6.

The Capture

NATTY TRACKER SAT in his computer room and racked his brain. How did the ninjas know that the roof was his Achilles' heel? They had to have found out by computer. Natty watched figures flash on the middle monitor as his big computer ran through various combinations to find an access code. Tracker had rented a small shop and had an alarm system installed from the same company that wired his home. He then tied into the alarm company's computer through the phony business' alarm lines. He was trying to get into their files to see if he could find out about his own installation. With a beep, his screen flashed "C:> \ ALRM.FLS," and Natty was into their files.

He started searching their files, and all of a sudden, a complete diagram of his house, grounds, and alarm system appeared on his screen.

Above the three computer monitors were six video screens showing the various views of Tracker's house and grounds. Feeling a chill run down his spine, Natty looked at all six screens, but everything was still and quiet. Inside the telephone transfer box hooked up to Tracker's computer, an electronic switch with a microchip and radio transceiver planted there by one of the ninja-garbed infiltrators was sending a signal to a receiver and microprocessor in an apartment on nearby Highway 115. A pair of oriental eyes looked at six video monitors and saw the same picture Natty was seeing. In the meantime, six super-VHS videorecorders played videotapes of Natty's house and grounds showing no disturbance there. The tapes had been made earlier and were now being played and transmitted to Natty's videoscreens.

Five minutes earlier eight black-clad intruders had pulled up outside Tracker's ivy-covered stone wall in a step van and had gone over the wall with a long aluminum ladder. They were now inside the mansion, and four were noiselessly closing in on Natty in his computer room.

Tracker glanced up at the six monitors again. Something was wrong, he sensed it. Natty looked at his wristwatch. It was noon. He looked at the monitors. The shadows of the bushes and trees in his yard were off to the side. At noon the sun was directly overhead. Natty jumped up and spun around. He saw a ninja-dressed intruder inside the room pointing an Uzi at him. Tracker dove as the gun spurted flames at his face. Then there was blackness.

• • •

He was making love with Fancy on a boat docked at Tripoli, Libya. Miguel Atencio shot her in the face and then aimed at Natty. Atencio turned into a ninja. Something was wrong here. It came to Natty: he was dreaming. His automatic defenses came into play, and he kept his eyes closed as his mind came alert. Tracker knew he was in trouble. The top of his head ached and burned, but he didn't know how he had gotten hurt. It was difficult for him to think. Natty could hear foreign voices in the room. Japanese, they were speaking Japanese. Jaki Kurikawa . . . he thought of her and remembered Hank and her capture.

Natty could feel that he was standing, but his head was hanging down. He barely opened his eyes and saw that he was totally naked and tied to a post. There was blood all over his chest, stomach, and legs, apparently coming from his head wound. Head wounds bleed a lot. He remembered that from somewhere. He looked left and right without moving his head and saw that he was in a dark, dank old building. He was tied to a post and to his left, about ten feet away, was a dirty closed window. He could see a narrow alleyway and another building with a window opposite but a little bit lower. The space between the two buildings seemed to be about eight to twelve feet.

Tracker slowly raised his head and saw four men sitting around a card table about twenty feet away. All were dressed as ninjas, and suddenly it came back to him. They had somehow breached the security of his house, and one of them had shot at him. Natty thought a minute. He felt weak and confused. He had apparently been shot in the head, the bullet creasing his scalp.

From behind, someone grabbed his hair and jerked his head back. Natty heard him speak in Japanese, and the others got up and came over to Natty, picking up guns on the way. Tracker pretended to be barely conscious as the ninja from behind confronted him.

He lifted Tracker's head and spoke in broken English, "Pretty soon, Tracker, you die. You talk, I promise you die fast. How you know about woman want kill you?"

Tracker moaned slightly and his head fell forward in a feint. The man lifted his head again and grunted. The head fell forward. Natty thought about how he could escape. He heard the group walking away, and he chanced squinting his eyes open a little. The entire group went back to the table and started talking.

Natty's left ring finger had been cut off while being tortured in Libya. Now he used his right hand to unscrew the prosthetic nylon finger in which he kept survival secrets. He let a little plastic ball and a scalpel blade fall into his hand. Holding the items in his left hand, he screwed the fake finger back on and then, using the blade, quickly cut through his bonds.

While the ninjas were looking away, Natty carefully reached up and pushed on his eyebrow and zoomed in through the window across the alley. He zoomed back out and then did a check of his legs and feet by flexing his muscles. Satisfied, he threw the plastic ball toward the table. It exploded, and Natty ran to the window and dived headfirst just as bullets tore after him. He felt a bullet burn his left calf as he crashed out the window. Sailing across space, he crashed through the other window and tumbled amid a pile of cardboard boxes. Natty automatically rolled to his left, split-seconds before a fusillade of bullets tore through the window behind him and crashed into the walls and floor.

The building was pitch black, but that didn't bother Natty as his electronic eyes had a night vision capability. He ran to the exit stairway and padded barefoot down the stairwell. After going down three floors, Tracker emerged on the ground floor. The building smelled like the inside of an old coffin, and Tracker thought of this as he saw eight shadowy figures appear outside the building.

He whispered to himself, "He who hesitates gets his nuts shot off."

With that, the nude hero ran across the darkened warehouse and launched himself at a black shadow walking by one of the dirty windows. Crashing through, Natty's shoulder struck the ninja on the neck, and his beefy arm wrapped around the man's head. The two crashed into a car parked along the downtown street, and Natty slid across the trunk with the ninja's neck, snapping it in the process. Natty quickly grabbed the Uzi off the man's limp shoulder and spun it, just in time, to spray two of the hit man's cohorts with a quick burst of searing bullets.

Still completely naked, he ran out in front of an oncoming car, pointed the Uzi at it, and held up his hand for the car to halt. The Pontiac Bonneville screeched to a halt, and Natty ran to the driver's door, jerked it open, and ducked just as several more ninjas appeared and fired bursts at him. He popped up and fired, knocking one down and sending the others for cover.

The driver huddled in a ball in front of the passenger seat as Natty jumped in and tore off down the road under a hail of gunfire. As he slid around the corner, he saw ninjas scrambling toward some parked vehicles. The passenger, wide-eyed and crying, sat up in the passenger seat. It was a ravishing redhead with a figure that would have made Madonna contemplate suicide.

Natty smiled, "Excuse me, I normally don't dress this way when I'm out for a ride."

She stared at him with a shocked look on her face. Then it dawned on her that he was joking. Wiping her tears, she started laughing uproariously. Tracker grinned and started laughing himself. Bullets tore by the car, and they both looked behind them to see two vehicles giving chase, ninjas firing out the side windows.

The woman laughed even harder and squealed, "Now we're going to be shot to death!"

She kept laughing as Natty tried to speed up and avoid the pursuing killers. Despite this, her hysterics kept Tracker laughing also.

Still howling with laughter, she said, "Well, at least if we get killed, you don't have to worry about getting bullet holes in your clothing."

GREEN LIGHTNING

Natty grinned and slid the car sideways to the right around one busy corner and back to the left around the next. He looked over, and she had begun to cry again.

Between sobs, she said, "Are you a killer?"

Natty laughed and replied, "No, I was kidnapped by those people and they were planning to kill me. They still are."

The young beauty thought for a minute and said, "I believe you."

Natty looked down at his bare body and grinned, "Why not? I'm telling you the naked truth. My name's Natty Tracker."

As he screeched around another corner, she held her breath and closed her eyes.

The car smoothed out and she replied, "My name's Deeann Light, but folks call me Dee."

Natty looked in the rearview and said, "Hang on."

He slid the car around another corner, tires smoking like they were on fire. Dee looked back as he quickly pulled over to the curb, and she saw two distant police cruisers speeding toward them, lights flashing and sirens screaming in pursuit. The two cruisers pulled up behind Natty, and the officers got out cautiously, hands on their pistol butts. All four of them walked toward the car slowly as Natty held his hands up inside the car so they could see that he wasn't going to shoot. He also saw two sedans roaring down on the policemen from behind.

Natty rolled down his window and leaned out, yelling, "Look out!"

The two cars of ninjas opened fire on the police officers. A short gun battle followed, but the cops, taken by surprise, were slaughtered.

Natty shattered the windows of the ninjas' cars and took off, tires squealing. He looked in the rearview and saw the ninjas piling into the two police cruisers. Tracker turned, sped down an alleyway, and slid out into a one-way street and headed the wrong direction, running oncoming cars off the road, and then he slid right around the next corner. Natty saw that he was in downtown Colorado Springs, so he knew the streets well.

"We'll go to my house near the Broadmoor," he said. "They've already seen your license number, so you're in danger if you go home."

"Can't we call the police?" she asked.

"You saw what happened to four innocent cops just now. They won't come to my house, because they'll figure I'll already have help there."

"Who?" she asked.

"The Army, the Air Force, whatever," he said.

"Who are you?"

"Just a man," Tracker said.

Tracker looked over and caught her looking down at him. She got very embarrassed and covered her face.

Deciding to lighten things up, Natty asked, "Are you okay?"

She got a concerned look on her face and responded, "I'm scared, but I'm okay. What's wrong?"

GREEN LIGHTNING

Natty grinned, "Oh, you were just looking a little cockeyed."

She turned and looked into Natty's eyes and the joke suddenly struck her. Her face got as red as her hair, and she buried it in her hands, laughing.

"I like your name," Natty said. "Dee Light."

In minutes, they were within several blocks of Natty's mansion. Natty halted the car and stared at the big house. He pushed on his eyebrow while Dee gave him a questioning look from the side. The house and grounds were quiet, and Natty spotted an African-American in a non-descript business suit. He figured this would be either a secret service man or an FBI agent, probably called in when Wally Rampart discovered that Natty had been shot and abducted. Natty drove forward slowly, however, still cautious. Three houses down from his house, he was spotted by a large burly man who waved him over. Tracker pulled over to the curb.

The man said, "I watch you being careful, Tracker. Those men are FBI. I called after you were carried out by Japanese."

"Thanks, Yuri," Natty said. "Why did you call?"

Yuri grinned, "Détente."

Natty laughed and gave him a wave and pulled up to his gate.

"What was that all about?" Dee asked. "Who was that man?"

"He's a KGB spy. The Soviets keep a group of

spies in that house—so they can keep an eye on me."

Dee was shocked now and asked, "Who the hell are you—James Bond?"

They drove to the front of the large house and Natty smiled over at her and replied, "Nope, just an average guy. You'll be safe here."

Feeling relieved and a little mischievous, Dee purposely looked down at Natty again and said, "Oh, Tracker, you don't look average to me."

It was Natty's turn to blush as she giggled. They exited the car, and amid stares from several shocked male and female FBI agents, they calmly walked into his large house.

Wally Rampart came storming out of Natty's kitchen, cigar clamped between his teeth. A shocked look on his face, he walked over to Natty.

"What the hell?" he fumed. "Look at your head. Are you okay? What the hell happened?"

Natty grinned, "Hi, General, I'd like you to meet my new friend . . ."

"I'm delighted," the Undersecretary of State said, hardly paying any attention to the pretty redhead.

"So is she," Natty said, still grinning and heading for the stairway. "Mind if I put on some clothes?"

Walking up the big staircase, he chuckled, "I'm going to keep my clothes on. Every time I take them off, I seem to get attacked."

Dee yelled after him, "I bet you do!"

She got embarrassed as she looked over at the

GREEN LIGHTNING

old walrus, General Rampart, and realized how forward her comment was. He poured a glass of brandy from a nearby snifter and handed it to her.

Wally said, "Here, young lady. I rather imagine you need this."

"Thanks," she said and quickly downed the brandy.

Realizing how right he was, the full impact of the ordeal hit her and she started to cry. She quickly caught herself, however, but not before Wally put a big beefy arm around her and sat her on the couch. Dee slowly sipped another glass of brandy and started to tell the old war horse what had happened.

Showered, shaved, and head wound cleaned, Tracker reappeared in a camouflage jump suit. He wore a leather harness with two Glock 19 nine-millimeter automatics in shoulder holsters. With a round in the chamber, each "little plastic gun" held eighteen rounds. Several different pouches were attached to the leather webbing, and there was a razor-sharp knife sheathed upside-down on the right chest strap of the harness. Natty set a small box down on an end table. With Wally grinning and Dee staring, jaws agape, he unscrewed the end of his left ring finger. Natty reached into the box and pulled out a new scalpel blade and explosive ball and put them into the finger and replaced it.

"Who are you, Robocop?" Dee asked.

Natty smiled, "Nope, just an average guy."

Wally Rampart started chuckling, "Yeah,

Tracker's an average guy. And Bo Jackson is an average athlete."

Looking at Dee, Tracker smiled warmly and said, "You can't go home. You can stay here, and they'll protect you."

"You haven't even asked me if I'm married or involved," Dee responded.

Natty grinned broadly, "You aren't."

Slightly irritated, Dee said, "How do you know?"

"I can just tell."

"How?" she asked.

"Several things," Natty replied. "One, you didn't have a second set of car keys on your key ring. Number two, I found out your address when I went upstairs to change, and if you were driving where we met at that time of night, I figure you had finished a date with somebody and didn't really want them to know where you lived. Besides, I've seen the way you've been looking at me."

Exasperated, she said, "Why, you conceited . . ."

Grinning mischievously, Tracker walked out of the room followed by a chuckling Wally Rampart. Dee started smiling after the two men left the room. They returned shortly deeply engrossed in conversation.

Wally said, "What makes you think they're still out there?"

Tracker replied, "They want me bad, so they're bound to be a few blocks away watching all lines of escape. I want to go out and find them."

"Then what?"

"Simple," Natty replied. "I have to lead them away from civilization. We don't know anything about Green Lightning. We don't know why they've been after me. I have to catch us some prisoners."

Wally agreed. "You're right there. So go out and get them to chase you, and we'll catch them with the FBI."

"No, we can't," Tracker said. "They've already shown they don't care about others getting hurt, plus they'll just take cyanide capsules if you catch them. It's got to be my way."

Wally thought for a minute and then said, "You're right, Natty, but you keep your head up and your ass down."

"Don't I always?" Natty said with a wink and a smile. "You know another thing: I can interrogate these guys and find out what we need to know, but you don't have as much freedom."

"You're right. You're right. What are you going to take?" the undersecretary asked.

Tracker smiled broadly. "Oh, just a little vehicle I've been working on. I better get going."

Wally gave Natty the thumbs-up sign, and Tracker walked over to Dee. She lost her breath with excitement as he scooped her into his muscular arms and gave her a long, lingering kiss.

He stepped back and whispered, "I'm sorry I got you into this mess. I promise I'll straighten it out when I get back. They'll get you anything you need. Call in sick for work and just stay here and enjoy."

She smiled up into his powder-blue eyes and

said softly, *"I'm* not sorry you got me into this. I'm glad."

Natty stepped back and looked into her smiling face.

She gave him a smoldering, sexy look and said, "Don't worry. When you come back, I have a feeling that I'll straighten it out."

Tracker looked into her eyes and volumes were silently said between the two. He smiled again and walked out, heading for his eight-car garage.

Several minutes later, with Wally and Dee standing on the big front porch of the mansion and several FBI agents looking on, the left door of the massive garage opened, and a low, powerful rumbling sound emanated from deep within its concrete bowels. A jet-black, customized Corvette Sting Ray, vintage 1969, slowly rumbled forth, sounding like it was almost ready to stall because of the three-quarter race cam in the modified 454-cubic-inch engine. The high-performance car slowly idled forward and stopped in front of the porch. The big powermill had been stroked and bored, had solid lifters and oversized pistons. It was fueled by a supercharger, or blower, and fuel injection. The interior had advanced instruments and state-of-the-art electronics. Tracker had also installed some added surprises.

Wally walked down to the car and the passenger window hummed down.

"You be careful," the old general growled. "The FBI will sweep this place lock, stock, and barrel.

They'll find any and all bugs those bastards planted."

"Thanks," Natty said. "Better have them let the Colorado Springs police and the El Paso County Sheriff know what I'm in and that I'll be drawing them away from here. See you when I get back."

Tracker rolled up the window and pulled away. He headed on a direct route for Highway 115, a main thoroughfare that passes by the main gate to Fort Carson. Natty thought about likely surveillance spots and eased toward the first one. Zooming in his eyes, he spotted a new Trans Am with three of the Japanese henchmen in it. Tracker turned onto a cross street, went down two blocks, turned into a dirt-covered alley used primarily by trash trucks and went down its length very slowly for several blocks. He emerged one block behind the ninjas and crept up slowly behind them. They were so intent on watching for him that they never looked behind them. When Tracker was almost even with them, he raised a small plastic gun. All three ninjas had their hoods off, so as not to arouse suspicion. The windows were down.

As Natty pulled alongside, the driver turned his head and looked into his eyes, complete shock on his face.

Natty grinned and fired, and a plastic dart flew out of the gun, the rubber suction cup striking the killer squarely in the forehead and sticking there.

Natty said, "Hi."

With a roar and a squeal, the black sports car shot forward while the surprised assassins started their car and took off after him. Tracker laughed as he looked in his rearview and saw that the driver still had not removed the dart from his forehead but was now speaking into a cellular phone. Tracker was glad. The killers had communication, so he would turn right on Highway 115 and head south, away from the city of Colorado Springs. They would follow him, and there were stretches on the busy highway where he could take them out if the traffic wasn't too heavy. Natty laughed as he saw the man finally remove the dart.

The other car was two hundred yards back, and Natty kept that distance between the two cars so he was relatively safe from their weapons. His idea was to get them away from civilization and let their friends catch up. What he hadn't figured on, though, was that they also had a helicopter. That helicopter was now revving up on a helipad less than twenty miles away.

Five miles down the road, a third Trans Am showed up in pursuit of Tracker's Sting Ray. The time was ripe, Natty decided, to go into action, except that the traffic was too heavy. Tracker also didn't want to discourage the killers so much that they would give up the chase. Then he thought about it and concluded that nothing he could do would make them want to give up the chase if they were fanatical enough to take cyanide when captured.

An explosion erupted in the highway in front

of Natty. His quick reflexes came into play, and he whipped the car around it, quickly downshifted into second, and popped the clutch. At the same time, he stomped the accelerator and whipped the wheel to the left, braking the tires loose and spinning the sports car around to face the direction from which he had come. He saw an armed helicopter coming at him. Natty was astounded and wondered how anybody could have gotten his hands on an armed helicopter and managed to operate it in US airspace. It was definitely not a US military helicopter.

The lead Trans Am was coming on fast, and two ninjas were leaning out the windows, firing at Natty. He quickly pushed several buttons. The headlights of the black Corvette swiveled, and Tracker looked at the oncoming Trans Am on a Heads-Up Display screen in front of him. A red light came on with a buzzer and the screen read LOCK ON. Natty pushed a button and twin computer-guided gatling guns spurt out a burst of flame from both sides of the front fender. Every fifth round was a tracer bullet, and each gun fired 8,000 7.62 millimeter rounds per minute. The Trans Am and its occupants were all but disintegrated within seconds. The other two cars slammed on their brakes and stared in disbelief.

Natty didn't have time to watch, though. He jammed the gearshift into first, popped the clutch while accelerating, spun the car around, and took off south as another rocket exploded where the car had just been. Driving down the highway with the helicopter in hot pursuit, Natty pushed more buttons, and the tail lights rolled up into the body. A tiny nylon dome came out of one of the openings and a video-type camera lens emerged from the other side. Several hollow tubes were next to these two instruments, but they were stationary, recessed in the car's body. Tracker now looked at the helicopter flying behind him on the computer screen. The screen had a shaded border around it, and the chopper remained in the upper part of the shaded border. Natty watched it on video and radar, which could keep it in sight. The hollow tubes contained high explosive rockets, but they could not be moved. The car had to have its rear end pointed directly at the target.

Tracker was now winding through a series of rock-walled canyons on a road paralleling the boundary of the Fort Carson military reservation. He was near the impact area where tanks, aircraft, and artillery live-fired for practice, so the firing of the rocket would not attract much attention. Tracker picked up his phone and called Wally and quickly explained the situation. Wally called Natty back and told him that two electric jets would be airborne within minutes. Electric jet is an Air Force slang term for the small but powerful state-of-the-art F-16. These marvels of modern weaponry are among the most maneuverable and deadly aircraft in existence. Tracker's challenge was to live through the next minute, then worry about the one after that.

A deafening explosion rocked the Corvette as another rocket slammed into the pavement next to it. A sheet of Kevlar made up the body of the customized car, as opposed to the normal fiberglass, and this protected Tracker from the shrapnel. He zigged and zagged the car along the highway at 135 miles per hour. The two Trans Ams were now nowhere in sight.

Natty knew he couldn't make it until the F-16s arrived without divine intervention. He had four rockets and he had to consider several things simultaneously. Should he fire all at once? Where could he fire them so they would safely explode in the impact area in case of a miss? Could he position himself to line up with the chopper?

Not far ahead, the road dipped down and turned to the right at the same place. That would be the only time Natty could attempt such a thing.

He decided to fire all four at once and go for broke. The turn was coming up, and Natty tried to make himself an inviting target but swerved the car left or right every few seconds to avoid a direct hit. He made the turn, headed downhill, and for a brief instant, the chopper appeared in the clear target area on the video monitor. Tracker pulled the trigger labeled FFE for Fire-for-Effect and watched the chopper give a frightened jerk as the rockets sailed harmlessly by it. Tracker's heart sank, but only momentarily, for he was a fighter and not a victim. He had to figure out another way to win. At his home, Dee and Wally were pacing the floor, but Wally was smart enough not to call Natty right then.

Tracker's face lit up as an idea hit him, and he floored the accelerator. He looked at the speedometer—150 miles per hour. He'd ease off on the gentle curves, although the car's anti-sway bars and positraction rear end were paying for themselves. The helicopter pilot, not knowing there were no more rockets, was now flying to Natty's upper left, and someone was firing out the door at him with a machine gun. Several bullets hit the car but the Kevlar body deflected them to the ground. The car topped out on a hilltop, and Natty downshifted several times while slamming on the brakes. The car skidded to a halt while the helicopter shot past it. Tracker grinned, because his gatling guns weren't stationary. They locked on a target and constantly moved with it. He quickly locked on and fired, and the chopper exploded in a ball of flames and debris, showering Highway 115 with bullet-riddled body parts and pieces of metal.

Just then, two F-16s roared overhead and dipped their wings in acknowledgment to Tracker.

Tracker spun the Sting Ray around and headed north on Highway 115. He knew what he'd have to do now. Within minutes, he came in sight of the two remaining Trans Ams moving slowly and cautiously forward. He aimed the gatling guns at a tree fifty yards to the right of the lead car and fired a very short burst at the tree. He slammed on his brakes. As he figured while he spun the car around again, the two cars started their pursuit again, the drivers thinking his gatling guns had malfunctioned. He kept his speed just fast enough to make them work for it but not fast enough to run away from them. This continued until Natty reached US Highway 50 and took it

GREEN LIGHTNING

west. Within minutes, the three vehicles roared through the tourist town of Canon City and continued on into the Rocky Mountains.

The cars passed between the steep rock walls of the Arkansas River canyon while the whitewater rapids of the angry river churned off to their right. They passed small groups of bighorn sheep on the sides of the sheer cliffs along the river. Occasionally the ninjas fired at Natty, but for the most part, it was all they could do to negotiate the winding two-lane highway.

Twenty-seven miles west of Canon City, Tracker turned south on Highway 69 at a little place called Texas Creek. He climbed uphill on the winding road and twice had to veer around mule deer crossing the road. Five miles later on, he emerged in the Wet Mountain Valley, and before him lay a setting that is one of the most scenic in the world. To his front and right lay the Sangre de Cristo Mountains. Thought by many to the be the prettiest and most majestic chain in the Rockies, most of the peaks were 13,000 or 14,000 feet high and all were snowcapped.

Natty drove south about 90 miles per hour with the Trans Ams still in sight in his rearview. He came to a sign and a store on the left side of the road. The sign read: BUY THIS TOWN, HILLSIDE, COLORADO—FOR SALE. Natty made a quick right and headed for the snowcapped peaks rising just a few miles in front of him. The cars roared up the old country road. Natty saw some elk grazing with a herd of cows off to his left and about fifty mule deer in an alfalfa field to his right. A gray- and red-coated coyote ran in front of him and Natty struck it with his front bumper sending the tough little animal whining through the air. It hit the ground and limped off. Natty headed down the right fork of the road, getting rougher now following signs that read: RAINBOW LUTHERAN CAMP. He stepped on it and pulled ahead of the Trans Am. The road finally became too rough and rocky so Natty slammed on the brakes. He jumped out and ran forward as he heard the killers approaching.

Natty grinned while he ran and said to himself, "Now, I've got you where I want you, assholes. This is my home . . . the wilderness."

Natty heard their cars stop and the doors open. He turned and fired in that direction hoping to hurry their pursuit so they wouldn't stop and try to trash his car. They didn't. The would-be ninjas hurried up the road after the handsome spy. Always in incredible physical condition, Tracker found the thinner air at 9,000 feet not too much different than what he was used to at 6,000 feet-plus in Colorado Springs. He knew, however, that, very shortly, as he continued to climb higher on the wooded switchback road, he would start to feel the altitude. He also knew that if *he* felt the altitude, the Japanese punks would *really* feel it. Tracker detected movement above him and saw a porcupine high in an evergreen chewing the bark away. He kept climbing.

Reaching into a side cargo pocket in his trousers, Natty pulled out a miniature smoke grenade cannister, attached a black string to the ring, and wedged it in the fork of a bush. He ran the string across the road and tied it around a tree trunk, then took off at a dead run up the trail, passing a lake on his left. A sign indicated that it was named Rainbow Lake. Tracker slowed his trot to a walk and laughed as he heard a burst of automatic weapons fire. Pretty soon, looking back, Tracker laughed again as he spotted some green smoke filtering up the side of the mountain.

He passed another lake and was now getting close to the timber line. Large patches of snow appeared under dense stands of pine, and breathing became more difficult. Natty looked down at the ground and at his tracks. He started running again and jumped up under an overhanging branch, grabbed it, and pulled himself up. He climbed out onto another branch, jumped to a branch in the next big pine, and repeated this procedure for five more trees. He then lowered himself onto a long, fallen tree, walked its length, and lightly stepped down, ball of the foot first, and crept away on the carpet of pine needles. Careful not to disturb them, Tracker climbed higher and higher until he finally emerged above the timber line. He was chilly and out of breath and at around twelve thousand feet elevation, which was exactly what he wanted.

Tracker started following ridgelines heading toward the south. He stuck to the opposite crest of the ridges to keep him from being silhouetted against the clear blue, cloudless sky above him. He was now walking on crusted snow patches at times, but Natty wasn't worried about being followed. He crawled to the base of a peak which gave him a view of a giant bowl below, and he scanned for the would-be ninjas. Tracker saw them walking along the road still looking for his non-existent tracks.

Natty laughed to himself as he watched the henchmen. He thought about the real ninjas who had lived centuries before in the days of the Samurai and knew that they would be better equipped to come after him. Because of numerous movies and publicity, nowadays many supposed bad-asses were wearing ninja outfits in an effort to disguise their true natures; they were punks and assholes. The real ninjas did most of their killings with poison as opposed to the more dramatic use of the martial arts, throwing stars (shurikens), or nunchaku (nunchucks or karate sticks). Not softened by city living, Natty thought, at least the real ninjas could have functioned in the wilderness.

He stood on the peak and emptied a magazine from the Glock 19 at the six exhausted hoodlums. They ducked for cover as Natty laughed and started heading southward along a ridge purposely letting them know which way he was heading. He looked to the northeast and saw the western slope of Pike's Peak and thought about his warm, comfortable mansion on the other side of the mountain near its base.

Tracker walked for a while, then moved out of sight and decided to watch the killers down below. He would catch up with them later on, but in the meantime wanted to keep track of them. He felt pressure pushing on his sinus cavity and

GREEN LIGHTNING

it was hard to breathe if he walked fast, but Natty loved the pristine beauty up so high. Down below he zoomed in on a beaver carrying a stick in his mouth to a new dam site.

The ninjas entered a patch of woods about fifty acres in size, and no sooner had they entered, than Tracker saw a cinnamon-colored black bear and two cubs emerge from the far side of the woods and run into a large dark evergreen forest. The big sow stopped at the wood's edge, stood on her hind legs, and swung her head from side to side. Zooming in on her, Natty could make out her powerful nostrils flaring as she smelled her enemy. Five seconds later he saw a very large old bull elk trot out of the trees and head off in another direction, into thicker woods, his large rack of antlers laid back across his back. Tracker grinned as he realized the unsuspecting ninjas would have no idea that they had spooked these animals. He watched the killers for an hour before moving on to a new vantage point.

Once there Tracker held his sides and rolled around laughing as he watched two of the hit men below get in a fight with each other. He saw a gun flash and one fell dead. Seconds later, he heard the muffled report of the gun. Natty saw the apparent leader walk up to the shooter and pull his gun from his hand and then backhand him across the face. He then gave the remaining thugs a five minute angry lecture, and the group marched southward into the woods.

Natty grinned and made a mental note that the

leader was the tallest and stockiest of all the killers.

He then unscrewed his fake finger; the scalpel and plastic ball fell out into his hand. Natty held up the stump of the finger where a small electronic device was attached to the base of it. Tracker reached down into the end of the prosthetic finger and pulled a thin metal wire out. He plugged the end of it into the electronic device in the finger's stump and dropped it over the cliff's edge. The wire uncoiled from inside the nylon finger and the finger fell down about eight feet. Natty spoke into the device on the end of his half-finger.

Wally Rampart's voice came back from the finger, "Tracker, you've got the Big Cigar, I'm hearing you five-by, over."

Tracker replied, "Cigar, Tracker. Hey, this is working pretty good. You want to have their cars picked up? Mine, too? Over."

"Wilco," Wally replied. "Are they parked where you were planning on? Over."

"That's a big Rog. We're up above and they're as inept as I figured," Tracker responded. "They left the vehicles in a hurry, and only one was wearing gloves, so I know you can get lots of good prints. Over."

"Great, okay, you be careful and give me a shout when you're ready for extraction. Over."

Natty replied, "Wilco. Out."

He wound the wire up around a little stick, pulled the stick out and stuffed the wire back into the end of the finger. He replaced the ball and scalpel and screwed the fake finger back onto the stump. Tracker then headed off toward the south, keeping an eye out down below for the ninjas.

A half-hour later, he spotted them again. They had stopped in a small clearing and were building a fire. The leader was not with the group, however. As soon as Natty noticed that, he heard a faint burst from an Uzi. A few minutes later, he saw the leader emerge into the clearing with a very small doe mule deer over his shoulders. It was time to move down the mountain, Tracker decided. The ninjas thought they were going to get a night's sleep. Natty thought differently.

Three hours later, under the cover of darkness, Nathaniel Hawthorne Tracker lay in mountain meadow grass just outside the circle of light from the ninjas' campfire and watched and listened to the men. Natty listened to them talk in Japanese and wondered what they were saying.

The leader said, "*Karada ga darui desu. Ashi ga itai desu.*"

Another said, "*Kimochi ga warui desu. Seki ga tomaranai n desu.*"

Natty crawled away, ate some beef jerky, covered himself with pine boughs and took a nap until after midnight.

In the darkness, Tracker crawled near the campsite. The five had built the fire up and curled into balls around it with their ninja hoods still over their heads. Tracker built a large fire about fifty yards away and then carefully moved the logs and sticks from their fire to it. He sneaked back and covered the rest of their fire with dirt and buried it completely. Having cut a large piece of sod from the edge of the meadow, he carefully placed this "lid" over the dirt covering their old campfire. Natty moved the deer carcass and each one of their weapons to the other campfire and carefully policed the area to remove any remaining signs of his trick. He then crawled away into the nearby pines and waited.

An hour later, the ninjas started waking and shivering. It took only seconds for them to realize that their fire was blazing away fifty yards from where they had all been sleeping. They gave each other blank looks, questioning looks, and just plain goofy looks. The leader got up and, after relieving his bladder, picked up a large burning stick from the fire and walked back to where they had been sleeping and scoured the ground, but not being an accomplished tracker, he could find nothing out of the ordinary.

Natty watched safely from a distance and kept chuckling to himself. He decided if he got the leader out of the way, the rest would be easy pickings. Four of the ninjas curled up in a ball and tried to sleep around the new fire while one stood watch. Natty zoomed in on close-ups of each ninja; they stayed awake for a long time, frightened eyes opened wide and looking all around. Tracker moved off into the woods; he had more preparations to take care of.

Two hours later sunrise peeked over the foothills. Natty lit a candle in his hidey hole and warmed it. He looked out from under the lid made of woven branches with carefully cut patches of sod on top. One hundred yards away, past the last of the trees and out in the meadow, the five ninjas were putting out the fire.

Natty saw them pointing directly at him, but he knew they had asked the leader which way to go and he had indicated the game trail that went directly south through the dark forest. The spider hole that Natty had carefully and methodically dug and camouflaged was right next to the trail. He had placed a small dead branch between the lid and the trail to keep any ninjas from stepping on it. The spider hole had been used by the Viet Cong during the Vietnam War. Usually the VC would dig a series of holes right next to a trail and cover them with a camouflaged lid of woven branches, leaves, and sod. The VC would stand in a deep hole in the ground or sit on dirt seats dug into the side of the hole. When a patrol walked by, the VC ambushed the patrol by firing almost straight up into their bodies from point-blank range.

The patrol headed toward Tracker and he extinguished his candle. A warrior in the tradition of his native American ancestors, he would now not feel cold or heat or pain until he accomplished the mission he had set for himself.

The five men walked by his spider hole and none of them heard a sound. Five minutes later, the patrol halted and the leader noticed that the last man was missing. They all gave each other worried looks and the leader called out for the man. Unconscious men cannot answer however, especially when they are several miles out of earshot and bound and gagged. They searched for the missing ninja for two hours and then gave up and headed south.

Below the snow caps of thirteen-thousand-plus-foot Spread Eagle Peak in the Sangre de Cristo mountain range lies a bowl filled with crystal clear beaver ponds, aspens, and towering evergreens. Here in the black woods are herds of elk, hiding from hordes of frustrated hunters spread out along the Rainbow Trail below. Here in this scenic bowl are timberline mule deer bucks with antlers that spread apart wide above the head and are as thick as a man's forearm with five or six or seven tines jutting skyward on each side of the head. Here in this bowl are landlocked rainbow and cutthroat trout in clear blue glacial ponds. In the summertime, big storm clouds bump up against the mighty crags on the western San Luis Valley side of the range and sometimes drop their snow or rain along the giant rock ridges before retreating down the steep western slope of the range. Some of the slopes hold graveyards filled with giant skeletons of mighty evergreens fallen head downward after having been bowled over by tremendous avalanches. In the base of the valley, young trees lay on their sides facing every direction like giant children's pick-up sticks.

On this valley floor, Tracker sat on one of the logs and talked to a would-be Japanese assassin whose head barely emerged from the grass-covered ground. The man had tried to be brave, but fear was apparent as he struggled to move his arms, legs, and body, held in by the suffocating dark brown earth. The remains of the young deer the head ninja had killed leaned against the back of the man's head, and its blood and grease had been spread all over his face.

"You know," Tracker said cheerfully, "bears, coyotes, buzzards, and crows all have several things in common. One thing is that they all cruise this valley constantly for food. They all have cast-iron stomachs, too. They'll love the remains of that deer you guys ate—and anything close to it."

The man stared at Natty, wide-eyed, as Tracker got up and started to leave then stopped and said, "You know, I figure you guys are sworn to secrecy and won't talk, so I'll just leave you here. If a bear or a coyote comes up, just yell and it will scare them away. Well, it will for a little while until they realize you're helpless. See you."

Natty turned and walked away at a fast pace but was halted by the man's yell. "Wait! Please come back! I talk!"

Tracker walked back, a big grin spreading on his face. He said, "You better be serious. If you tell the truth and I believe you, I'll give you a chance to live. Any lying or hesitating and you become a meal."

"I won't lie! Please!" the man screamed pleadingly.

Natty sat down on the log and said, "What is the name of your organization?"

Without hesitation the ninja replied, "The Ryoku Rai Kyookai."

Natty said, "Wait a minute."

The prisoner stared, jaws agape, as Natty unscrewed his finger and prepared the little radio, called Wally Rampart and had him tape record the interview.

"Okay," Natty said, "again, what is the name of your organization and what is the English translation?"

The man repeated, "The Ryoku Rai Kyookai and it means the Green Lightning Society."

"Is it part of the Yakuza?" Tracker asked. "And what does the name stand for?"

"It is because they use computers to steal money. The 'lightning' is for electronics and the 'green' is for money," the frightened man answered. "No, we are not part of the Yakuza. We are much richer."

"Who is the head of the organization?" Natty asked.

"I don't know," the man replied. "I have not seen this man. I have just heard that he is very big."

"You mean rich and powerful?"

"No, I mean he is very very big . . . and mean."

Tracker realized that this man could only provide limited information since he hadn't even seen the head of his crime syndicate. He asked just a few more questions and called the coordinates in to Wally who already had a helicopter on the way loaded with FBI agents. Tracker took off after the other killers even before the helicopter arrived.

Some miles to the south of Spread Eagle Peak lies a steep-walled mountain called Marble Mountain and above the timber line is a cavern entrance called the Caverna del Oro. The cave entrance is only accessible during the latter months of the summer. The rest of the time it's covered by heavy snow. When it was discovered a suit of armor from a spanish conquistador was found at its entrance with an old and weathered arrow sticking through the part covering the heart. An old cross was found painted on a nearby rock marking the proximity of the cavern entrance. Inside, spelunkers discovered vertical shafts dropping several hundred feet and the remains of a giant windlass, reputed to have been used to raise and lower millions of dollars worth of spanish gold bullion. Further down the mountain lay a giant rubble of boulders from a rockslide which supposedly covers the main entrance to the Caverna del Oro. Legend has it that the innards of Marble Mountain hides millions or even billions of dollars in Spanish gold bullion. Near the upper cave entrance are the remains of an old Spanish fort, supposedly erected by the conquistadors to fight off the Indians who had been pursuing them.

The Caverna del Oro is an area that's steeped in history and controversy, and this was the spot Natty Tracker chose to capture the remainder of the gang of hit men. The previous night, Natty had kept them awake all night with various harassment techniques and then knocked out and carried off the leader one hour before daybreak while the rest, totally exhausted, were fast asleep.

The man had been interrogated and hauled away by chopper. All that Natty had learned was that the RRK used computers by infiltrating employees into businesses and stealing computer access codes. They would then use the codes to execute swift and complicated switches of existing funds, moving them from one account to the next until they ultimately arrived at the RRK corporate account in Tokyo.

Three ninjas remained and they were now hungrily devouring a snowshoe hare after not having eaten for over twenty-four hours. A small plastic ball flew from the trees and landed in the midst of the campfire and quickly exploded. Sparks and ashes flew everywhere, one ember catching the black-hooded shirt of one of the ninjas on fire. He screamed and pulled the shirt off quickly and tossed it aside while the others fired blindly into the forest. All three were frightened and angry and cursed loudly in Japanese.

The firing stopped and the whole setting became deathly silent. The three stared into the dark wood, straining their eyes to catch a glimpse of the unseen enemy. The one without his shirt started to shiver, so he took five steps to pick up his shirt. It was gone. He stood and his heart pounded heavily in his ears. It was not even night yet, and this man had somehow sneaked into their camp and had spirited his shirt away while they stood there staring into the woods in all directions and looked for him. The killer got another shiver that ran up and down the length of his spine, but it was not from the high country cold.

He turned and relieved his bladder while his eyes wandered everywhere. Tracker held his breath as the warm urine splashed down on him through the interwoven branches above the spiderhole. He had planned well and was such a good tracker he had picked this as their potential campsite ahead of time. His grandparents had taught Natty well. They taught him to follow a track and figure out how the person or animal would think by the signs along the trail. Tracker had watched these men for several days and saw what type of terrain they selected for their campsites and he had planted a phony, easy-to-read trail right to that very campsite. Several strategically placed logs and a bush attached to the woven lid to the spiderhole had kept them from stepping on the lid.

With the patience inherited from his red forefathers, Tracker sat still in the damp, dark hole and allowed the smelly urine to air-dry in his clothing as he waited for nightfall. He used the man's shirt and hood to dry his face, neck, and hair. Natty concentrated on the visualization of a tiger walking through a hot, steamy jungle. Every time his mind started to wander, he forced himself to recapture that image. He mentally focused on the animal's muscle and sinew, the rich colors, and the symmetry of its movements.

Natty thought to himself, "Tiger, tiger burning bright in the forests of the night. What immortal hand or eye formed thy fearful symmetry?" He tried to remember the poet and where he had read the lines and then caught himself and concentrated on just visualizing the scene again.

He breathed through his nostrils and tensed his toes and the balls of his feet then totally relaxed them. Next he did the same to his heels and ankles, then his calves and knees, his thighs and buttocks, his stomach muscles and lower back, his chest and upper back, his fingers and hands, lower arms, upper arms, then his shoulders and neck, and lastly his face muscles. Finally Natty relaxed his entire body and pretended it was melting into the bottom of the hole. He slept peacefully within arm's reach of his enemies.

At midnight, Tracker awakened, carefully lifted the lid, and looked at the campfire. Knife between his teeth, he slithered out toward the crackling embers. The bare-topped man lay close to the fire, arms wrapped around his naked torso and curled into a fetal position. All three slept soundly.

Natty laughed to himself thinking of all the would-be ninjas and supposed assassins. Tracker had much disdain for groups of self-proclaimed "hard-asses" such as the Hell's Angels and was always amazed how untough they became when not part of a large group. Natty was a hero because that was part of him just like being part Native-American, part Norwegian, and part African-American. He was truly a man and had little patience for those who weren't but tried to disguise it with what he called "human wolf growls."

"Nobody fucks with me!"

"You fuck with me, you better sell your soul to God 'cause your ass is mine."

"You better not fuck with me, son, because you're dealing with a man now."

These were just a small example of some of the many phrases Natty Tracker referred to as "human wolf growls." He had no respect for the phrases or the men who spoke them, or for those who tried to dress like or imitate ninjas, soldiers, or anybody else who was considered macho. He now saw three men who fancied themselves as trained, disciplined hit men, but Natty regarded them as three frightened little boys who were lost in the woods. Working in urban settings, the three men had eight murders-for-hire between them, but out on Marble Mountain they were in Tracker's home: the wilderness. Out there they were defenseless mice and Natty was a scarred old hunting cat. Batting them first this way and then that way, he would finally devour them after they trembled enough to sufficiently amuse him and sate his appetite for justice.

He slowly crawled to each hit man and checked his breathing. He judged the oldest-looking one to be sleeping the soundest. Tracker slowly and methodically cut away the man's shirt with his razor-sharp knife. He then cut away the man's pants and crawled back to his hole with the clothing. He dropped it in and waited and watched, but the man just curled in a tighter ball and scooted toward the warm fire. Natty crawled back to the fire, added a few sticks, and then cut away the third ninjas clothing and the bare-topped killer's pants. After depositing his new trophies in the spider hole, he crawled back and cut away the men's shoes and socks. All three men stirred slightly but were probably too exhausted from their ordeal so far to awaken.

Not yet satisfied with his mischief, Tracker again snaked his way back to the fire and carefully took an Uzi from one of the killers. He emptied the magazine letting the bullets drop onto the grass. Next, using his knife, he pried the bullet from the brass casing and poured out the gunpowder. He then pulled a metal box from his pocket, and took out a small plastic explosive ball like those he carried in his fake finger, and dropped it in the shell. Natty replaced the bullet and then reloaded that and the other bullets into the Uzi. Following that, Tracker repeated the same procedure with the other killers' weapons. He then crawled into the blackness of the nearby forest.

Positioning himself behind a large tree, Tracker stuck one of his Glock 19s around the bulky trunk and quick-fired the entire magazine into the air over the campfire. The three men came out of deep sleep in an instant, realizing they were naked as they blindly fired their weapons in the direction of Tracker's muzzle flashes. As each weapon fired on the sabotaged bullets, almost simultaneously, the three weapons exploded and two of the three ninjas fell on the ground, screaming in pain. The third fell on his back, sightless eyes staring up at the clear night sky, a jagged piece of metal protruding from the bridge of his nose. The other two held their arms and sides while writhing and moaning over several minor, but painful shrapnel wounds. Tracker suddenly appeared on the other side of the campfire, a nine-millimeter in each hand and a smile spreading across his handsome face.

"Looks like you three got a big bang out of my little surprise. Why didn't you give up a couple days ago and head back to Tokyo?" Tracker said.

One of them responded, "We cannot go back. If we fail to kill you, we will die in disgrace."

"Okay," Natty replied cheerfully, "I'll let you two go, and you can keep trying to kill me."

"No, no," they both responded simultaneously.

One of them went on, "We do not want to pursue you any further."

"I'll tell you what," Natty replied, "I don't have to play by the rules. I can kill you out here and make you suffer as much as I want. We already interrogated your friends and they broke. They are alive and are going to stay that way. Now, I'm going to ask you a few questions and you will both live if neither of you tells me a lie. If one of you lies, I'll shoot you both in the knees and elbows and leave you out here. I'll know the answers to some of the questions and can compare your answers with those of your buddies. Both of you think about it for a second."

Tracker sat down by the fire while both men examined their wounds.

Two minutes later, he said, "Who is the man that ordered you to kill me and where can he be found?"

The two men looked at each other and then the previous speaker responded, "He is called Ken Furoshiki and he can be found at the Shotokan in Tokyo. He sometimes teaches there but usually picks out people he wants to fight."

Natty grinned and the man went on, "Even you do not want to fight Ken Furoshiki, Tracker."

"Why?" Natty asked.

The man grinned at the other and spoke to Tracker, "In Japan he is called *Shinkansen*."

Natty asked, "What does that mean?"

"The Bullet Train," the other replied. "Because he is so big, fast, and powerful."

A helicopter approached as Natty stood, smiled, and said, "A little crowbar can derail an entire train."

7.

The Shinkansen

THE JAPANESE POWER lifter lay on the weight bench and raised his tree-trunk arms. Sweat trickled in small streams off of his massive pectoral muscles as his hands took hold of the American-made York barbell. Other lifters gathered around, and a murmur went through the crowd as the two spotters lifted the 560-pound barbell off of the rack and held it over his chest. Rosin fell from his hands and drifted lazily down onto his massive bulk of muscle and sinew as he cautiously nodded to his spotters. They released their grip on the bar and it descended toward his chest; he yelled as it touched the skin, and he strained to push it back up. Onlookers cheered him on, and his eyes nearly closed as he summoned up the last bit of strength to make his arms fully extend and elbows lock. They locked just as he felt his veins would explode and his chest and heart pop from the extreme exertion. He yelled for his spotters to take it and a hush fell over the crowd. He looked up to see two huge hands sweep his spotters away, and a single massive hand grabbed the bar in the middle and helped set it on the rack. He dropped his arms, sat up, and looked into the cold, cruel eyes of The Shinkansen.

Ken Furoshiki had a chest that was muscled like a stocky roping horse. The bastard son of a Japanese mother and a gargantuan-sized Mongolian who had deserted the Red Chinese Army and had eventually ended up in Japan, Ken had been the by-product of a brutal rape. He stood six feet eleven and weighed four hundred and eighty-five pounds. He held black belts in Shotokan karate and Kodokan judo, but did not have the attitude of the normal martial artist. The Shinkansen had studied at the Shotokan, the Japanese national university for the study of karate.

His favorite pastime was to hang out and watch the best fighters. He would then pick out an exceptionally strong, tough fighter and follow him for several days. He did this to instigate a fight so he could kill a capable warrior in hand-to-hand combat. It would not be an exaggeration to say that Ken Furoshiki was probably one of the top five toughest, most dangerous men in the world in a fight to the death without any weapons. Most of the people he challenged simply and sensibly backed down, but if the Shinkansen picked that man out as a potential opponent, it was difficult to escape his challenge. He would rape the man's wife while the man was away and then stand over her bed until the husband returned home and eventually kill them both with his hands or feet.

When the hierarchy of the Ryoku Rai Kyookai learned of this sadistic monster, he became the number one man to head their "maintenance squads." They referred to their thugs and henchmen as maintenance squads because they were used to identify and repair any problems with their so-called "white-collar" operations. The RRK cadre thought that by calling their killers maintenance squads they were making themselves look nicer than the gangsters they were.

On Ken's eighteenth birthday, after five years of searching, he finally found his father. His father's face was crisscrossed with scars from battles and barfights over the years and he stood six feet six. At the time, Ken was two inches shorter than his final height. He confronted his father about deserting him and his mother before he had been born. His mother had never told Ken that his father had raped and impregnated her, but his tough old man told him with a laugh and a sneer of disgust.

During the subsequent fight, Ken literally tore his father's head from his shoulders. After killing his own father in the short-lived fight with a crushing blow to the head that snapped the tough old man's neck like a matchstick, Ken grabbed at the windpipe and pulled and twisted until the flesh finally tore away. He used that as a starting point and continued to pull and tear until the head finally tore free of the body. He salted it and carried it home in a plastic trash bag to his mother in Tokyo. He proudly presented the trophy to his mother and was surprised when she screamed in shock and horror. He, however, was experiencing his proudest moment.

Ken was paid a million dollars per month by the RRK to recruit and manage the members of the syndicate's killing gangs. It was certainly a profitable job but not a challenge to him. He constantly needed an adrenaline rush. He almost went after Tracker himself when the assignment came down, but he had a deathly fear of flying, so he had opted to stay in Japan.

It was midweek when the American arrived at the Shotokan and started observing classes. The man had been asking around for Ken Furoshiki and had already spotted him. The Shinkansen followed him through downtown Tokyo to an exclusive restaurant that specialized in Kobi beef. The world famous Kobi cattle were kept in tiny individual corrals. Each day, a trainer massaged each steer's entire body and the animal was allowed to drink only beer, not water. The steaks from these steers are world famous and are shipped to the finest restaurants in many countries. Ken stood in the alleyway across from the restaurant and waited for the tall dark American to come back outside. The American had black hair, a dark complexion, and stood about six feet four.

An hour later, the man emerged from the restaurant and headed for his rental car. The Shinkansen slipped back into the alley, swallowed by its eerie darkness. He started moaning, and the man, hearing this, headed cautiously into the

GREEN LIGHTNING 107

trap. It was a dead-end alley, and the man discovered it too late. He had already passed by Ken who had been hiding in a black doorway and stepped out blocking the only possible escape. Even in the partial shadows of the alley, the Shinkansen's size and bulk was unmistakable.

The man said calmly, "Well, Mr. Furoshiki, I wondered when you'd finally spot me."

Furoshiki spoke with a gravelly voice, "I spot you long time ago, Mr. Tracker. Now you will die."

The tall American laughed, "Sorry to disappoint you, friend, but my name's not Tracker. Name's Clem Wiseman, CIA, and I'm afraid I'm going to kill you. I've already faxed all kinds of files about you and sent tapes of you to Tracker. They warned me about you and I just won't fuck around."

Clem Wiseman was definitely not a wimp. He had served three tours in Vietnam as an infantry squad leader and platoon sergeant with the Americal Division and the Big Red One, the First Infantry Division. He went back to the "World" with several medals and was sent to the Army's intelligence school at Fort Holabird, Maryland. Two years in a brigade S2 shop sold him on being a "spook." After he put in his twenty for the army, he immediately went to work for the CIA, wanting to "travel to exotic lands, meet interesting people, and kill them." That is exactly what he had planned for Ken Furoshiki as he pulled a Colt Python .38 Special from a shoulder holster.

The humongous Shinkansen chuckled in a low growl as he walked slowly forward.

"Sorry, Pal," Clem said, "I don't need karate."

Clem unloaded all six shots from his .38 into the massive frame of the Japanese assassin. Before Vietnam, he had been an assistant NCOIC at a .45 automatic pistol range at Fort Benning, Georgia, and could consistently fire expert with a pistol even on his bad days. His six shots at the Shinkansen could have been covered with a silver dollar, but the giant barely staggered and kept coming. Clem's mouth dropped open as he stared up into the cold cruel eyes of the Oriental. Ken laughed and reached inside his shirt and pulled on two Velcro straps. He extracted a bullet-proof vest and held it up in front of Ken's face with a laugh.

Ken said, "Kevlar," and then laughed again.

The ball of his foot shattered Clem's ribcage with a vicious front kick, and the CIA operative flew backward into a brick wall, his head making the sound of a watermelon being thumped hard. Ken's follow-up right hand reverse punch completely smashed Clem's face, and he wavered and fell face down on the dirty asphalt, quite dead.

The Shinkansen bent over, picked up the Kevlar vest, and walked out of the dark alleyway.

In Langley, Virginia, and in Colorado Springs, Colorado, quarter-inch tape recorders rolled with nothing but static coming from the speakers since the initial kick shattered the microphone and transmitter taped to Clem's chest.

GREEN LIGHTNING 109

An intel analyst at CIA headquarters rewound the tape recorder and made a call to Natty Tracker's house, but there was no answer.

On the other side of the Rockies, Tracker looked out the window of his suite in the newly opened Las Vegas casino called The Mirage. Dee Light got out of the bed, walked over and wrapped her slender arm around his muscular waist and watched out the window with him. They saw cars and pedestrians moving up and down the dizzying street full of lights and neon signs named Las Vegas Boulevard but called "The Strip" by locals and tourists alike. Between them and The Strip stood beautiful trees and palms, gorgeous pools and cascading falls, and a dome-shaped man-made mini-volcano. Water erupted from the dome as red and orange lights shone upward through it.

Tracker turned and kissed Dee while the red and orange lights played on the sides of their faces. His fingers traced little trails over her smooth skin. She shivered as his fingers started at her buttocks and ran lightly up her spine. She felt his excitement pushing against her and breathed in short excited breaths. Natty had not been with a woman who excited him so much— and so often—in a very long time. Dee was a class act. A patent and copyright attorney, she was intelligent, independent, and charming. She was also independent enough to allow Natty to feel like he was in charge and protective of her. The backs of his fingers ran lightly, very lightly, up over her shoulders and along her neck under her ears. She took a deep breath and started bending at her knees with her lips sliding down his copper torso. Tracker's beeper went off.

He walked over to the nightstand and looked at the number on the digital pager. He was to call his answering machine. He called and received the message from CIA headquarters. Half an hour later, Natty and Dee were in a white stretch limo on their way to Nellis Air Force Base where his Lear jet was safely hangered under guard. Natty refueled at Burbank Airport and again at Honolulu where he left Dee, against her protests, at a fancy resort hotel. He was able to operate all of the gadgetry in his computer center by remote control, so he listened to the tape playback of Clem's death in the cockpit of the luxury jet. Tracker didn't know Clem very well, but that didn't matter. Ken Furoshiki was going to die— after he talked. Natty had the tapes of Furoshiki transmitted to a three-quarter-inch machine in the plane, and he watched the killer over and over while he soared across the blue Pacific.

Tracker set the jet down at Yokohama Air Base and smoothly guided it onto the tarmac. Lear jets are piloted by two people, so Natty left his copilot with the aircraft to guard it. The copilot, Jim Elias, had been a cargo pilot for Air America, a long-known arm of the CIA. He had flown F-100s in Vietnam and flew cover during the Grenada invasion. Jim was not only Natty's copilot but was working for the CIA as well. He had been assigned to Tracker which he didn't mind, because most of the time, Natty either flew his single-person aircraft or worked on some project on the ground. That way, Jim could concentrate on his personal life, something he hadn't done for years, and still make a salary of almost six figures. His wife and two teenaged daughters were happy to finally have him at home most of the time. They understood that he sometimes had to leave with less than an hour's notice and might be gone for days, but it was much better than it had been for many years when he would be gone for a year or more at a time.

Tracker took a taxi to an American-owned hotel in downtown Tokyo. The following afternoon, he took a taxi to Camp Oji on Tokyo's outskirts and walked through a gate in the ivy-covered walls past two white-gloved MPs and into the main administrative building of the US Army's Seventh Field Hospital. He was directed to a smaller one-story building near the back of the compound which was labeled CAMP OJI OFFICER'S OPEN MESS. He entered the building and was immediately greeted by a smiling Wally Rampart. Several doctors and a female nurse sat at the bar and eyed the two civilian men with some suspicion. Wally took his beer and a Blackjack on the rocks for Natty to a small round table in the corner. Both men sat down in overstuffed chairs.

"The President doesn't like you coming here after Furoshiki," the Undersecretary said. "He says we have plenty of qualified people that can take him out without risking you."

"The President is not my boss," Tracker replied.

"He is right now, Tracker," the general growled. "You're on assignment."

Natty chuckled, "Look, General, when are you guys going to learn to let me handle things my own way without the babysitting?"

Wally swallowed hard on his bottle of Miller Lite and shoved a cigar in his mouth.

"Yeah, you're right," he finally said with resignation, and that closed the matter.

Changing the subject, Natty, asked, "How did you get here so quickly?"

"I was in another country."

Tracker dropped it just like that, knowing that Wally Rampart had other classified jobs to perform besides babysitting him.

Wally pulled a sheaf of papers from his briefcase, tossed them on the table, and said, "Here's what you asked for—Furoshiki's house. Even tossed in a copy of his blueprints for you."

Tracker picked them up and glanced at them with a simple, "Thanks."

Wally asked, "Does it have what you need?"

"Where does his electricity come from?"

"It's there in the second or third photograph: an electric line runs outside his house and a tie in wire runs from the transformer on the pole in front of his place. . . . Just out of curiosity, what are you planning on doing to Furoshiki?"

Tracker laughed and said, "Oh, that's simple enough: I'm planning on beating the shit out of him."

Wally Rampart spilled the remainder of his beer on his lap as Natty laughed much harder.

GREEN LIGHTNING

* * *

It was about two o'clock in the morning when Ken Furoshiki was awakened by a noise in his large house. He jumped out of his specially built, double-king-size four-poster waterbed, slipped on his karate ghi trousers, and went searching for the source of the noise. The realization suddenly struck him that nearly all the lights in the house were on. The Shinkansen carefully searched the entire house but found nothing, so he went back to bed.

An hour later, he was awakened by a noise in his spacious master bathroom, and he jumped up, turned on the lights, and ran there only to find the bathroom window open, curtain flapping with the breeze. The lights in the house were still off, so he turned on the bathroom light, closed the window, and then used the commode. He started to leave the bathroom, but something caught his eye, and he stopped and stared into the bathroom mirror. A chill ran up and down his spine. Written on his forehead in bright red lipstick was the Japanese word SHUTEN. It is a railroad term, making reference to his nickname of The Shinkansen, and it literally means "the end of the line."

Furoshiki had a large karate dojo, or gym, built onto his mansion and he heard noises coming from it. He quickly ran downstairs to investigate and again found the lights on in the whole downstairs. Opening the door to his dojo, Ken Furoshiki was greeted by the sight of Nathaniel Hawthorne Tracker in a sweat-soaked black silk karate ghi, practicing an intricate Tae Kwon Do kata. A kata is a choreographed form using various kicks, blocks, and punches in a particular pattern of movements. He could not believe the gall of this intruder, but he just stood and stared as Natty finished the kata and then bowed.

Tracker grinned at the Herculean oriental giant and said, "Name's Natty Tracker, Mr. Furoshiki. You should have worn the top to your ghi. Hard to hide behind your Kevlar vest without it."

With a roar, The Shinkansen flew forward at Natty Tracker with the speed of Carl Lewis, the determination of Lawrence Taylor, but the size of Andre the Giant. Natty did a side-escape and spinning hook kick to the behemoth's ribcage but barely fazed Ken with the technique. Furoshiki countered with a front snap kick and set the foot down in a front stance and followed with a powerful reverse punch, but both techniques missed. This is the most common one-two fighting combination used by Shotokan stylists and Natty knew this very well.

Tracker started dancing around and stung The Shinkansen with two flashing backfists to the left temple. Tracker faked a third backfist and fired a powerful sidekick to the floating ribs off his lead foot, but Furoshiki almost shattered the shin bone with a sweeping downward block. The bone and muscle were badly bruised, and Natty felt that it hurt so badly his grandfather might have felt it. He danced again to try to shake off the pain.

Ken came at Natty in a modified front stance, faked the front kick, and caught Tracker with a left hand reverse punch that Natty partially slipped. If he hadn't slipped it, the force would have shattered his skull. Furoshiki, trying to outdo the famous Japanese black belt Mas Oyama, had already killed two full grown bulls with both a left and a right hand reverse punch to the forehead. As it was, the punch caused Natty to see stars, and he danced away as he shook his head from side to side to clear his skull. The Shinkansen got a very evil grin on his watermelon-sized face as he moved forward, knowing his foe was hurt. Tracker laughed just to unsettle him.

The two martial artists faced each other sideways in backstances. Tracker lifted his lead arm just two inches. Ken saw Tracker's arm a little too high to effectively block a fast kick to the base of the ribcage. His right foot shot out with a lead-foot sidekick. Simultaneously, Natty dropped to the floor under the outstretched sequoia-sized leg and shot the blade of his left foot upward into the exposed groin of the monster. As the air left the Shinkansen's mouth with a rush of pain and shock, Natty swung the same foot back and viciously roundhouse kicked the back of the giant's left calf right on the nerve meridian, and the brute crashed heavily onto his back.

Miraculously, Ken Furoshiki was on his feet as quickly as Tracker and was facing him with an evil, sadistic leer. Natty knew this was a ploy and saw the pain the man was really feeling by staring into the killer's eyes. He also saw insanity there.

"Now, Tracker, you will die," the Oriental said with a cavernlike voice.

Natty got a big grin on his face and replied, "Is is true that giants have tiny dicks?"

With a roar, the monster rushed at Natty again and Tracker side-stepped and lashed out with two lightning roundhouse kicks to the groin in less than a quarter of a second. This time the giant doubled over holding his groin.

Natty laughed and taunted, "I'm having a ball, Kenny. How about you?"

With another roar, the six-foot-eleven-inch killer attacked Natty Tracker with a nonstop series of kicks and punches that Natty tried to slip and block, but every time his body made contact with Furoshiki's it rocked him to the bone. It was then that it really hit home with Tracker that one slip, one missed block, one slight miscalculation, and he was a dead man.

"I don't care now," Furoshiki said with a mad look in his eyes, his head lowered. "I don't care now."

Curious, Natty said, "You don't care about what?"

"I don't care if I'm hurt. I don't care if I die, too. I will kill you now and rip your head from your shoulders," the madman replied.

For the first time in years, Natty experienced real fear. A warrior, though, he knew the three states of mind that will defeat a warrior in a fight are fear, sympathy, and ego. Tracker cleared his mind and started grinning again to upset Ken even more and make him fight foolishly.

GREEN LIGHTNING

Natty said, "I knew if I'd kick you in the groin enough that you'd go off half-cocked."

The Shinkansen, murder in his eyes, stalked forward, fists doubled. Natty smiled broadly while he reached down in his ghi pants. He pulled out a small box that looked like a miniature garage door opener. He shook his head and pushed the button. All the lights went out and the room was immediately pitch black, except to Natty Tracker with his daylight-quality night vision. He immediately started stabbing the Japanese assassin with quick jabs and kicks. Frustrated, the big man went into short bursts of rage and panic and swung blindly, but Natty easily stayed away from the ham-sized fists and feet. Finally, the Goliath started swaying, and Natty, standing off to the side, quickly lashed out with a quadruple roundhouse kick to the kneecap, groin, solar plexus, and lips. He set his foot down and lashed out with a knife-hand strike to the Adam's apple, crushing the windpipe. Not stopping, Natty grabbed the man's hair and shattered the bone under the left eyebrow with a reverse punch. He then jumped up and spun in the air with a jump spinning crescent kick that caught the brute on the left jawline and temple, breaking the jaw and sending him unconscious to the floor.

The Shinkansen opened his eyes and couldn't see anything. He made a mental note of his injuries and could tell that his groin was severely swollen, his jaw and cheekbone were broken, and his throat hurt so bad he couldn't swallow. Additionally, he knew he had several broken ribs, as it felt like a knife was sticking into him every time he tried to breathe. His legs were folded underneath him and crossed, and the apex of the shins folded over each other pressed against a post. Twine was tied around his wrists and had been pulled backward and was making the front thigh muscles feel like they were ready to tear in half. He also felt as if both knee joints were going to pop through the skin. The pain was the most excruciating he had ever endured.

The lights came on and he saw Natty with the small remote switch in his hand. His legs were wedged up against a post in the corner of his dojo. He looked back and saw that both wrists were tied with heavy baling twine and were stretched back to two blocks and tiny posts Natty had nailed to the floor. Tracker went back to the two little posts and took another wrap of the twine around each, pulling him back even farther. He screamed, and sweat rolled off of his face in buckets. Tracker didn't speak; he wrapped two more winds around the posts every few minutes while Ken Furoshiki screamed. He was bent backward almost to the floor with his arms stretched out behind him at an angle.

"What do you want to know?" the killer screamed.

Natty didn't answer. He just smiled, and this terrified The Shinkansen. Tracker got up and walked out of the room, reentering a few minutes later. He carried a handkerchief and a pitcher of water along with a roll of duct tape. Still in excruciating pain, Ken Furoshiki was totally unnerved.

Tracker pulled the handkerchief across the man's mouth and nose and taped it in place. He picked up the remote and switched off the electricity again. Ken's heart started pounding in his neck and temples. Tracker started pouring water onto the handkerchief, watching when the frightened man inhaled. Furoshiki gagged and gasped in total fear and panic. Tracker kept it up, not letting the man clear his lungs or catch his breath. When The Shinkansen thought he couldn't stand another teaspoon of water or another twist on the twine, Tracker stopped and the lights came on. Natty removed the handkerchief and duct tape.

Natty said, "I think you know by now that this is just a sample of what I can put you through to make you talk."

The assassin leader shook his battered head affirmatively.

Natty continued, "Should I get more creative, or do you want to save wear and tear on yourself?"

Resignedly, The Shinkansen said, "I will talk if you promise me a quick death."

Natty smiled. "Cross my heart."

The monster said, "My boss's name Yoshihisa Shibuya. He is president of large corporation name Green Lightning International. They steal much money. Big, big building. Address is 3-20 Konan, 3-chome, Minato-ku, in Tokyo. Building has giant sign on top of lightning. It is green. This is all I know."

Ken bowed his head while Natty left the room and returned a few seconds later. Tracker opened his hand and there was a pill in it. He put it between the man's teeth.

"I'm not going to kill you," Natty said. "That is your pill. You can swallow or spit it out. Your choice, big guy."

The man bit down and swallowed. Foam came out of his mouth as his body twisted. Natty started to walk from the room and looked back at the massive corpse.

Tracker said, "Looks like he bit off more than he could chew."

8.

The Dragon Had Breasts

TRACKER SWALLOWED A piece of ham covered with raisin and pineapple sauce and looked at the sexy bikini Dee wore across the table from him. He hadn't even gone back to his hotel room but instead took three different taxis and walked part of the way to the airport. The Lear jet sprang into the air in no time and headed for Hawaii. Tracker did not want to finish the war until he let his wounds heal from his battle with the giant.

The following day, he lay on a private beach at a CIA safe house just outside Honolulu while Dee massaged his muscles. In the afternoon, a helicopter flew in and took him to a naval hospital, and they discovered a slight concussion from the glancing reverse punch and a hairline fracture of the tibia from Ken's powerful block. Tracker didn't worry about the fracture, but he was smart enough to know he needed unstressful rest for the concussion or his brain could mess him up at a critical time, and he didn't believe in losing. He was also waiting for the intelligence agencies to gather some information on Yoshihisa Shibuya.

Before leaving Furoshiki's home, Tracker had left the RRK a powerful message. Natty had taken a black magic marker and drawn a series of tiny footprints on The Shinkansen's massive chest. He knew the RRK would realize that it was; "tracks" and there would be no doubt what the symbol meant. He didn't know how right he was; at that time, they had pulled out all the stops and would spare no expense to have Natty Tracker eliminated.

The RRK had billions of dollars and they would use whatever money necessary to locate and kill him. After seeing the photographs of the dead, tortured, and beaten mighty gargantuan, all the members of the RRK were terrified. Who was this mighty warrior who had felled their protector? What kind of monster could this American be?

Tracker looked across the table at Dee, and with a grin took the fragrant lei off of his neck and draped it over her bare shoulders.

With an impish grin, Natty asked, "You want a lei?"

She grinned, took a drink, and replied, "Love it."

That night they danced into the wee hours at a romantic club overlooking Pearl Harbor. It was the first time Natty had tried any exertion whatsoever since the fight, and he knew that his body was quickly healing. He wasn't supposed to dance with his walking cast, but Natty knew it wouldn't really hurt him. Besides, he figured it was well worth another fracture just to be able to dance with Dee. They looked at the moonlight blinking on the powerful breakers rolling in from the mighty Pacific, and he kissed her hard and long.

They returned to the safehouse around two A.M. and made love all night. Right before daybreak, Tracker led Dee down to the private beach, and they went swimming in the nude and continued their lovemaking. Natty had been kissing Dee, and she was still wearing one of her flowered leis. He started pulling it apart and lightly swirled the fragrant blossoms around her taut nipples and her pubic mound. He kissed her lightly and delicately all over and entered her as the waves occasionally ran up the beach to tickle their toes. They tried to make love slowly but were soon so overcome with passion they pounded against each other like the powerful surf. The ecstasy built and built and finally they both exploded, and so did the safehouse. The explosion was deafening and Natty threw his arms protectively over Dee's head and face and lay on top of her as debris rained down on and around them. Staying on top of her, Natty carefully slid her along the sand and down into the water. He led her as they both swam underwater parallel to the beach. Emerging behind some palms, they came out of the water and crawled up into the relative safety of the trees.

Tracker looked at her and smiled softly, seeing fright in her eyes.

He grinned and said, "God, honey, nobody ever

made me come like that. You really are *something*."

Dee stared at him and then broke into a big grin and blushed. She slapped Natty on his powerful bicep and then impishly pinched his bare butt.

"Now what?" she asked.

He looked down at their naked bodies and replied, "Well, first we probably ought to find some clothes. Remember what I said about what keeps happening to me every time I get naked?"

She teased, "Well, I'll say this for you: when you bang a girl, you do it in a big way."

"We have to watch the house for a while and make sure nobody's around," Natty said. "Besides, it probably won't hurt to let them think they killed me. In any event, I apologize. I shouldn't have taken you out tonight. It was too dangerous and I know better."

"I don't care," the beautiful redhead responded. "It's been scary, but I've never enjoyed life more than the time I've spent with you."

Tracker stared at her and they kissed passionately again. He lay on his back and she lay on top of him.

"If we need to keep away from the house and watch it for a while," she said, "we ought to figure out a way to kill time while we're hiding here."

With that, she placed her mouth over Natty's and plunged her tongue inside hungrily searching for his. They made love once more.

• • •

GREEN LIGHTNING

The morning sun shimmered on Dee's red hair as she looked on in amazement while Natty unscrewed the end of his finger, pulled out the antenna wire, attached it to the bark of a palm tree, and started talking into his finger. She was even more amazed as she heard Wally Rampart's voice crackle back from Tracker's finger.

Then it was Natty's turn to be amazed as he saw a veritable army of ninja-clad bad guys appear at the edge of the palms on the other side of the demolished safehouse. The killers stayed out of sight because the fire department and police had already arrived at the site. Natty, however, had spotted some movement and zoomed in on the black-hooded figures who were lying down behind trees and clumps of flowers, out of sight of the Hawaiian safety forces. Natty felt that to announce his own location would bring instantaneous sniper fire. He also knew the RRK was very, very wealthy and apparently wanted him really bad now. He had killed their champion.

He heard boat motors and saw several speedboats appear near the mouth of the cove.

Natty whispered into the tiny radio, "You wouldn't believe the army and navy of killers they have here closing in on me. You know the trees and gardens on the south side of the driveway? Over."

Wally responded, "Roger. Over."

Natty said, "There's got to be about fifty of those fake ninjas with automatic weapons hiding in there. You need to get a couple of jets and put an air strike in there. Over."

Wally's voice came back, "You're crazy. That's a civilian neighborhood, pal. What if a five hundred pounder falls short? No way. Over."

"You're right," Natty whispered back. "But they have more in boats and they're going to all close in when the cops and firemen leave. You also can't send troops or cops in. These guys are going to fight to the death—I guarantee—and they all have automatics. Over."

"Stand by, and don't worry. I'll get you out of there. Over," Wally replied.

Natty said, "Wilco. Out," indicating he would comply and the conversation was over.

Five minutes, which seemed to the naked couple like an eternity, passed and Wally's voice crackled on the radio again, "How about it Tracker? Over."

"Rog-o," Tracker replied.

"Guess what unit's been in Hawaii and are airborne on the way to you right now. Over," Wally asked.

"Gee, I don't know," Tracker responded half-joking and half-sarcastic. "Why don't we play twenty questions while I get my ass blown off? Over."

Wally's belly laugh came back clearly over the airwaves, "Now there's an idea that would save me a lot of headaches. Operation Black Knife's on the way. Over."

Tracker smiled broadly. "Fantastic, tell them to make one quick pass and come right back as soon as the balloon's up. I'll be in the suit and

GREEN LIGHTNING 127

will hold Dee. It has to be quick because I have no weapons at all. Over."

Wally said, "No weapons at all. You mean nothing? Over."

Tracker paused and cleared his throat. "We are totally naked and have nothing with us but air and sunshine. Over."

Dee started chuckling as Wally said, "Well, you damned sure won't be able to club them to death will you? Over."

Natty started to speak and just then Dee leaned over and said into the mini-radio, "That's for sure," and she fell over giggling hysterically.

Tracker goosed her and said, "Ha-ha, very funny, you two. I'm counting that they'll hold off because of the cops, but who knows? Over."

"Aw, don't worry. You get out of every tight spot that can be thrown at you. Over," Wally replied.

"Right," Tracker responded. "What do you think I'm speaking into right now, a Sony Walkman? Over. Oh, hey, I hear the plane. Tell them I'll lay on my back in the water to mark our location. Over."

"Good luck. Out," came the reply.

Natty carefully slipped into the water floating on his back in a spread-eagle position. Seconds later, a huge four-engine AC-130 Hercules Air Force cargo plane roared overhead and then banked out over the ocean in a wide circle. Natty slipped out of the water still unseen by the ninjas.

Dee said, "Natty, what the hell's going on?"

"Honey," he replied, "I'm sorry. There isn't time to explain. You've got to trust me and we have to move very fast."

"I do trust you."

The plane looked like a giant catfish, Dee noticed, as it came back toward them, as it had two giant pieces of metal sticking out from its nose like the whiskers on a catfish. It created a giant V and Dee tried to figure out if it was some kind of an antenna. Something came out of the plane, and a multi-louvered cargo parachute opened and a large green bag dropped to the ground, landing within ten feet of the duo. The cops and firemen stared as the naked Tracker ran out and grabbed the bag and dragged it back behind the trees. Two cops ran toward him, guns drawn.

They approached the grove of trees cautiously and came upon a broadly smiling Natty Tracker donning what looked like a military flight suit with an emergency parachute sewn onto the abdomen.

He smiled and said, "Have you officers ever been in a life-or-death emergency where you don't have time to explain anything?"

Behind Natty, a giant balloon, shaped like a blimp, was inflating from a hydrogen bottle in the bag. Tracker released the balloon and it started ascending skyward with a thick nylon line trailing out of the bag beneath it. The officers looked at each other questioningly.

One said, "Look, pal, I don't know what's going on here, but you'll have to come with us."

GREEN LIGHTNING

Natty said, "No time to explain, officers. I'm sorry."

"Sorry for what?" the other asked.

Just then the very voluptuous, very naked Dee Light stepped out from behind a tree. Both officers stared at her ample breasts, flat tummy, red love triangle, and athletic legs. She smiled seductively.

Natty said, "For this," as he skipped forward and kicked one in the temple with a flashing right foot roundhouse kick and immediately flipped the foot straight across in a hook kick to the other's temple. Both officers crumpled in a heap.

Natty winked at Dee and grabbed her. He sat down on the ground cross-legged and had her sit on his lap and wrap her arms tightly around his neck. He looked up, and his eyes followed the line all the way from the back of his suit to the blimp-like balloon. Below the balloon, two different flags fluttered on the line about fifteen feet apart. Tracker looked over and saw two cops, guns drawn, cautiously moving toward him. He heard the plane approaching again.

Clutching Dee tightly, he said, "Dee, put your head right next to mine. Cross your ankles and squeeze me tightly."

She complied, and three seconds later, the mighty plane passed overhead, catching the line between the two flags in its metal V-shaped nose device. The balloon was cut loose, and the line was grabbed at the apex of the V. Dee and Natty were pulled into the air about twenty feet and then suddenly zoomed into the sky trailing behind the plane on a long tether. A top secret device transferred the nylon tether from the front of the plane to an electronic winch inside the back of the plane where the line now trailed out the open tailgate. Tracker and the screaming redhead were winched into the plane's tail cargo door as they whisked through the Hawaiian skies at breakneck speed.

When they reached the ramp, the plane's crew chief leaned out and helped pull them in. He immediately supplied Dee with a faded green flight suit after filling his eyes with sensuous memories for many NCO club stories. Dee threw her arms around Natty and he held her as she cried hysterically for a full ten minutes.

Afterward, she collected herself and said, "Natty Tracker, there's no man in the world who could've gotten me to trust him as much as I just trusted you. I was so scared."

Natty smiled and kissed her on both eyelids very softly and held her tightly. When they landed an armed military escort helped them into a waiting limo and whisked them away.

The two were taken to a heavily guarded cinder block building. Inside, they found several desks and chairs, a television set, and a couch. They both lay down and napped for several hours until they were awakened by the gruff voice of Wally Rampart. Wally debriefed Natty and also presented him with a large file on Yoshihisa Shibuya.

Two days later, Dee found herself under heavy guard at a CIA safehouse in the care of an operative named Jay Silverbird. The house was disguised as a home garage service and was located in eastern Arizona on the Second Mesa Indian Reservation of the Hopi Tu tribe. Dee felt very safe there and was able to finally rest.

Natty, in the meantime, was back in Tokyo with a team of intelligence agents who were checking out every female psychologist and psychiatrist in the Tokyo area. They were trying to determine whom they could trust to compile more information about Jaki Kurikawa. After several days, they really didn't have much. Her slate was essentially clean. Tracker did learn that she traveled constantly, especially to America, and that her father had been under Yoshihisa Shibuya as an aide in the Japanese air force and he knew that both men had served in the Second World War.

Yoshihisa had been a general when he retired. After his retirement, he had gotten involved with the Yakuza, the deadly Japanese mob, and was one of the few people who ever left its ranks alive. He had apparently been a bit of a politician in the air force and that was how he had attained his rank. It was established that he had a bit of a gambling problem and owed money in Las Vegas, Atlantic City, and Monaco. He did pay his debts, but they were in the millions. He also was a very avid golfer with a four handicap.

Because of Jaki's numerous trips to the US, Tracker figured she was probably one of the main front people for pulling off their fund-switching scams. Further checking showed that she and her father had formed a Nevada corporation, using a Las Vegas attorney as the incorporating agent. The corporation was called Dragon Lady Inc. and bought small businesses, packaged them, and resold the businesses to large conglomerates looking to diversify. Dragon Lady Inc. apparently was a legitimate business and had offices on Maryland Parkway in Vegas. The offices were manned by accountants, attorneys, and a small staff who were experts at making "window dressing" out of balance sheets and annual reports.

Further research showed that a Delaware attorney had been the incorporating agent for Jaki and her father in an import/export business, named USBAPU International which reportedly imported and exported goods to Brazil, Argentina, Uruguay, and Paraguay. Tracker figured it was probably a front for drug smuggling with the idea that those countries would not be monitored as closely as Columbia, Peru, or whatever.

Natty also learned that, through the corporations, Jaki and her father had purchased estates throughout the United States, each complete with fine furnishings, elegant cars, and other amenities. The father had died, so Jaki apparently now owned everything. Tracker also wondered how many more corporations and assets she had that he hadn't discovered. He also wondered about how much money the Ryoku Rai Kyookai really did make with one of its middle-management people controlling such wealth and power. Tracker knew from what he had learned so far that she was far from being one of the top dogs in the RRK, so he was left almost breathless when he considered what the bosses must be raking in.

Natty decided on a frontal assault, so he went directly to Jaki's office complex which was in a high-rise office building not far from the Meiji Jingu Shrine. The crowd of people was thick outside the shrine, and Tracker's head and shoulders were conspicuously higher than those about him as he elbowed his way through the throng. He caught his breath and entered the modern building, located her name on the directory, and headed for the elevator. When Tracker entered her reception area, he smiled at a middle-aged receptionist, held his finger up in a shush gesture, and walked to the door of Jaki's private office.

He looked at the receptionist and asked, "Speak English?"

She nodded affirmatively and said, "Sure."

Natty said, "I'm an old friend and want to surprise her. Any patients in her office?"

The look of concern left the woman's face and she smiled, gestured, and said with a whisper, "Nobody in. Go ahead."

Natty winked and briskly opened the door and walked in, closing it quickly and quietly behind him.

Jaki was bent over in the far corner watering a large vase full of flowers and greenery. Assuming it was her secretary, she didn't turn but mumbled something in Japanese. Tracker took in the view and considered it gorgeous. So far, however, he had only been watching the doctor bending over.

He looked around the office and noticed the Western décor. The furniture and wall coverings were American Southwest in earth-tone colors. There was a Frederick Remington on the wall and there were bronze statues everywhere there was table space. The office was spacious and the windows were massive. A Navajo rug was draped over the back of the very expensive leather couch. On one wall there was a massive bookcase filled with leather-bound volumes, along with an expensive CD system, VCR, and large-screen Sony Trinitron.

Natty had to hand it to her. When she stood and turned to face him, she never changed her expression. She smiled and gave him a smoldering, sexy look.

She started unbuttoning her dress as she said, "I knew you would come someday, but I want you inside me before you try to kill me. No man has ever excited me before. But you—you are dangerous."

Natty didn't even speak as her silk dress fell away revealing one of the most incredibly shaped bodies he had ever seen. His pulse quickened, but he also remembered this woman setting crazy Hank James against him. He knew that something deadly was coming and all of his defenses were alert as he pretended to be taken in by her act.

Natty took a breath at the sight of her large firm breasts rising as she reached with both hands to pull the chopsticks from the bun in her shiny black hair. Tracker remembered seeing her wear-

GREEN LIGHTNING

ing two chopsticks in a bun when he saw her before at the Broadmoor, so on a hunch, he dived to his left. The dive saved his life as her arms whipped forward and the first deadly dagger whipped by his neck and stuck into the wall behind him. The other knife, however, got him directly in the right lung, collapsing it, and the shock caused Natty to see stars. Stay alert! he thought as he saw her quickly throw her dress on and run out the door.

Natty knew he was a dead man if he fainted now. He also knew that some gorillas were going to charge through the office door in minutes, if not seconds. He ran to the window and looked out at the ant city twenty stories below. He ran to the desk and opened it quickly. Tracker found what he wanted: a plastic file folder. He quickly covered his sucking chest wound with it. He then found some packing tape and made an airtight seal around the plastic patch's edges. He propped a chair against the door handle and looked out the window again. Tracker unscrewed his finger and tried to call Wally Rampart to explain the situation. The office had been soundproofed and was protected against electronic surveillance. Natty couldn't get through. He tried not to panic as his sight wavered and his knees buckled. He heard loud voices in the outer office. Somebody tried the door knob—or had they, he wondered? He slapped himself across the face and his mind cleared up.

Tracker grabbed the Navajo blanket off the back of the couch and gripped it tightly in both hands as a MAC-10 machine pistol chattered and splinters of the door flew through the room. Tracker ran, and covering his head with the blanket, crashed headfirst out the large office window. He fell downward for twenty feet and hit the flagpole sticking out from the balcony below with the outstretched blanket. His powerful arms absorbed the blow and he wrapped the blanket around the end of the pole and held tight. His body went past the pole and the fixture bowed sharply but remained affixed to the building. Natty couldn't waste time celebrating. As the momentum carried his body down and then in toward the building, he let go and flew another eight feet and crashed through the window in the office two stories below Jaki's. He curled into a tight ball, hit the floor in a roll, and plowed into the back of an overstuffed office chair. A distinguished-looking Japanese lawyer flew headfirst across his desk and landed, unhurt but shocked, on the floor. Natty moaned and stood up, weaving. He helped the attorney to his feet and forced a painful smile.

Tracker said, "Sorry, I'll use the door from now on."

He exited the room, leaving the attorney speechless, his jaw hanging open.

As Natty opened the door to the hallway a huge ninja armed with a sawed-off Mossberg twelve-gauge with pistol-grip handle suddenly appeared. Tracker dropped on his back, and the blast went over his face and into the lawyer's hapless receptionist, decapitating her on her twenty-third

GREEN LIGHTNING 137

birthday. Tracker's left foot pulled against the killer's left heel as Natty snapped out with a vicious kick to the man's kneecap with his right heel. The assassin's kneecap exploded with a loud crack, and he fell to the ground with a scream.

Tracker's hand closed over the man's trigger hand and pulled the gun away and swung it upward, catching the killer on the point of the chin with a powerful butt stroke that shattered most of his cervical vertebrae. Natty dragged the body into a hallway closet.

Several minutes later, ten ninja-clad punks took up firing positions on the building's ground floor as they watched the floor numbers of the descending elevator. They had shut off the other elevators and knew that Natty was now descending on this one. Several gulped as the number one flashed. There was a pause and the door opened. Tracker was pointing a gun at them and they all opened fire, simultaneously riddling his body with hundreds of bullets. Cheering, they ran forward and rolled his body, shot to rags, over. It was their tallest hit man in Tracker's clothes. The floor mop that had held his body up suddenly fell over and struck one man across the back. A shiny staple gun fell out of the corpse's hand.

Tracker popped through a door and onto the building's roof. He was dressed like a ninja and carried a sawed-off shotgun. The others had still not tried the roof ten minutes later when the US Army helicopter appeared overhead, Stabo rig trailing beneath it. The bottom of the rig had a T-bar type of seat and Natty climbed onto it as the chopper sped away. Barely conscious, Tracker felt the electric winch pulling him up toward the speeding helicopter. He unscrewed his fake finger and tied himself to the rig with the antenna wire. He fainted.

9.

With a Vengeance

TRACKER OPENED HIS eyes and looked straight up at a spotless off-white ceiling. He looked around and saw he was in a sterile room. A nurse walked in and a smile spread across her face as she looked at him. She started to run out the door to summon help, but was stopped by Natty's voice.

Tracker said, "Where am I?"

She smiled sweetly and responded, "Walter Reed Army Hospital, Washington, D.C."

Natty smiled and fell asleep.

The following morning, Wally Rampart came into the hospital, enthused about the news that Natty would soon be back on his feet. He walked into the heavily guarded room and saw the thin drapes flapping from the open window. He ran to the window and looked out but saw no one. Wally kicked the nearby chair and mumbled something obscene and then noticed a note on Tracker's pillow. He picked it up and read it:

Dear General,
Remember your promise: no more babysitting! I have some serious ass-kicking to do. I'll be in touch.

Tracker

Undersecretary Rampart stared at the letter, lit a cigar, then lit the note, and dropped it into the bedpan. He started chuckling and it soon turned into a belly laugh. He opened a briefcase scramble-phone and quickly dialed.

He said, "This is Rampart. Get a top secret order off to the CG of USSOCOM down at MacDill with a copy to the CG's of PACCOM and JFK Center. Tell them to get the First Special Forces Group on alert in Okinawa for possible deployment to unspecified areas in Southeast Asia. Have operational detachments standing by aircraft and make sure they have strong Japanese language capabilities. Send copies to appropriate Navy and Air Force support units. Run all of it by the Secretary of Defense and get his approval and put it all under his signature block. Tell the Secretary this is for Operation Green Lightning and should be top priority. Don't let anybody else in on this except on a need-to-know basis and all pertinent documents need to be labeled TS and hand-delivered. Got it all?"

There was a short pause and the general continued, "Okay, good enough. Later."

He hung up just as a very large matronly nurse walked in the door and got an angry look on her face.

GREEN LIGHTNING 141

She scolded, "You put that big rat dick out in this hospital! You understand?"

Chuckling, Wally handed her the lit cigar and scooted out the door, quickly looking right and left for the nearest EXIT sign.

A scorpion scurried across Tracker's bare copper leg, but Natty paid it no mind. Dressed only in a breechcloth like many of his forefathers, he sat on a flat boulder tinted red from the large amounts of iron in its interior. He stared for miles across the broad expanse of shimmering Arizona wasteland before him. Unmoving, he concentrated on his wounds and pictured waves of healing energy pounding into the injured areas and washing away the pus-filled tissue and leaving a residue of fresh pink cells.

He had gone to his grandfather and said, "Grandfather, I need help."

The old Indian took Natty first to a sweat lodge, and then after bathing, had the wounds cleansed and poulticed with the old roots and herbs passed down from shaman to shaman. The same remedies had cleansed the wounds of Geronimo, Cochise, Mangas Coloradas and many other great Apache leaders of the past.

A coyote crossed Natty's line of sight and disappeared behind a creosote bush. It passed a barrel cactus, some yuccas, and then out of sight among the rocks.

Tracker dropped his body across the warm rock and slept. He slept the sleep of his carefree childhood. A presence awakened him and his eyes opened instantly, all senses alert, but he smiled seeing the wrinkled, leathery old skin of his grandfather's face.

The gnarled old man said, "Tell me, young one, did you see a coyote run behind a cactus, a creosote bush, and some yuccas?"

Natty never ceased to be amazed by his grandfather.

Like a young boy, full of wonder, Natty responded with enthusiasm, "Yes, Grandfather, I did. Were you hiding behind me and watching?"

"No," the old man said calmly, "I was trying to repair the damned washing machine for your grandma."

Natty smiled and asked, "Then how did you know?"

The old man grinned. "You know that the sky-people and the Keeper of Dreams will sometimes talk to us through visions, young one?"

Natty sat up, wide-eyed, "Yes, is that what happened?"

"No, it didn't. Before you are many creosote bushes, barrel cacti, and yuccas. There are also many coyotes in this area. It is obvious that you would have seen at least one. It was all there before your eyes."

Tracker grinned broadly and shook his head.

His grandfather continued, "Did you see the rattlesnake which crawled towards you while you were watching the obvious?"

"No, I didn't."

"I didn't see it either," the old sage replied, "but I know that it was there. You have told me your story and I have thought of the battle before you. The danger will not be in the many coyotes you will see darting from bush to cactus, but in the snake which will be much closer, moving quietly in the shadows, poised to strike. You must be careful of this, my son."

"I will, Grandfather," Natty said.

As the twin Pratt and Whitney powerhorses shot Natty's F-15E Eagle across the Pacific Ocean, he felt renewed and ready for battle. After leaving Walter Reed Hospital, Tracker found himself weak, in much pain, and disoriented. He knew that he could heal much faster under his grandfather's care, so he went to him. For the first several days, Natty had the same feeling you have when you lean back too far in a chair and it just starts to fall backward while you quickly lean forward and grab for the edge of the table. He still felt some pains here and there, but knew that meant his body was healing itself. Tracker was ready for the RRK and their deadly little hit lady.

Jaki Kurikawa's secretary got a shocked, frightened look on her face when she raised her head and saw Natty Tracker standing in the doorway.

Voice trembling, she said, "Doctor Kurikawa is on leave of absence."

Natty said firmly, "Leave."

The woman picked up the phone and started to dial, but screamed as the blade of Natty's hand came down on the main part of the phone with a vicious shuto, a knifehand strike that shattered the instrument. She got up and ran from the room clutching her purse to her chest.

Tracker walked into Jaki's office and pulled a thermite grenade out of the cargo pocket of his trousers and pulled the pin after setting it on top of her filing cabinet. It started burning down through the files while Natty turned his attention to the rest of the office. He placed all the art objects in a large box and set them in the outer hallway. He then went back inside and fired his two Glock 19s through the office furniture. Pulling a knife from a sheath down his back, he slit the couch and chairs to shreds. Afterward, he took a fire hose in from the hallway and hosed down the burning files. After tipping over the ruined furniture, he destroyed the reception area. Natty walked out and retrieved the box of valuable art items and headed for the stairs. He walked down two floors and entered the law office where the receptionist had been killed. He passed the new receptionist with a smile and entered the grey-haired lawyer's office. The man was with a client and looked at Natty with a start.

Tracker said, "Told you I'd use the door next time."

He set the box down on the man's desk and pulled a roll of Yen out of his pocket and dropped it on the attorney's desk.

Tracker said, "Sorry to interrupt you. I want to hire you to give these art items to a reputable museum. Just say it's from an anonymous donor. Can do?"

GREEN LIGHTNING

The lawyer nodded affirmatively and Natty smiled as he left the room.

Tracker went up the elevator and emerged on the roof. There he mounted an invention of his he had first used to infiltrate Libya. Carrying it, broken down, in two break-apart pods under his jet's wings, Natty had assembled his Hovercopter and flown it to the building's roof. Made of lightweight materials and a small engine, not much larger than a lawn mower's, it was a combination one-man helicopter and one-man hovercraft.

Additionally, Natty had equipped it with an electronically controlled M-60 7.62 millimeter machine gun. Connected to swivel left, right, up, and down commensurate with Natty's head movements when he wore a specially wired flight helmet, it was fired by an electronic trigger mechanism in Natty's mouth. When he bit down on it, the gun fired six-round bursts.

On top of that, Natty had the barrels of four M-79 grenade launchers welded together which he could fire simultaneously or individually with foot-controlled triggers.

A large lever on the Hovercopter could be moved to put it into either the hover or the flight mode. In the hover mode, the overhead rotors were disengaged and rotors under the inflated vinyl tubing under the base turned like large lawn mower blades and air channeled downward raised the craft two inches off the surface. In the flight mode, the hover motor disengaged and the overhead and the tail rotors activated to lift and move the aircraft.

In the flight mode, Tracker revved the engine and whirred up into the sky above busy Tokyo, heading directly toward 3-20 Konan, 3-chome, Minato-ku, Tokyo, the corporate headquarters of the Green Lightning International Corporation. He wanted the head of Mr. Yoshihisa Shibuya and the other top management people. It took only ten minutes before Natty was setting the Hovercopter down on the building's roof.

He went through a door and down a flight of stairs. He went from office to office, floor to floor, only to find the building totally deserted. Some office furniture still remained, but for the most part, the entire business had rapidly moved out of its own headquarters building.

Twenty-eight stories of offices were now deserted, apparently because of a fear of Natty Tracker. It gave him an incredible sensation and an awesome feeling. Natty stopped and sat on some cardboard boxes in an empty office. Tracker thought about it; he had defeated The Shinkansen, a ferocious and probably assumed unbeatable foe. On top of that, Natty had defeated him in hand-to-hand combat in the man's own house. Tracker had defeated scores of hit men sent after him. He had outfoxed the psychopathic serial killer they had sent after him. Then there was the unbelievable escape from Jaki Kurikawa's office, and he had been wounded as well. Obviously, he had put the fear of God into the upper management of the Green Lightning Society, but it blew Natty's mind to think that one man could accomplish such a thing. The building was owned and had been built by the RRK and was actually quite modern and beautiful.

Checking the main floor, he found all the doors chained and bolted shut. The electricity was still on, but the air conditioning was turned off. Tracker took the elevator to the top floor, went up to the roof, and left in the Hovercopter.

After a visit to his hangared and guarded jet, Tracker returned after darkness fell. He again set down on the roof, and again made a floor-to-floor inspection of the entire building. This time, however, Natty was wearing a pack he had loaded at his jet. He went back to the roof and looked out over every side of the building. To the south side of the building lay a large vacant lot where an old building had been razed. Tracker saw three cars parked along the street by the vacant lot.

He went back down and kicked out the glass in the back door of the building. Tracker ran outside and pulled shaped explosive charges from his pack. He placed these on major bracing beams at the base of the building. He also pulled out blocks of plastic explosive and molded it against spots that looked like "cornerstone" areas. All of these were equipped with electronic detonators. Tracker then broke into the three cars and pushed them down the street into the next block.

It was one o'clock in the morning when Natty finally finished rigging the building and returned to the roof. He started up the Hovercopter and lifted off. Tracker made a sweep around the building, and seeing no one walking or driving toward the empty structure, he pulled out a small box with a detonator button and an antenna. He made sure he was far enough away and then pushed the button. It amazed Natty that such a little button could do so much damage. The explosives went off, and the south wall dropped straight into the street. The entire structure, all twenty-eight stories, fell across the street into the vacant lot with a mighty crash and a cloud of dust. By that time, the Hovercopter was well away from the scene. The cleanup would cost the city of Tokyo lots of money, but the police had quite a laugh about it.

Tracker next went to the homes of Yoshihisa Shibuya and six of the RRK's board members who had been finally identified with the help of the Japanese intelligence service and law enforcement agencies. The Japanese were well aware that Tracker was after the RRK, and they appreciated it and welcomed his efforts, as they didn't have to worry about their own officers risking anything. They had to assume that Natty was responsible for the complete destruction of the RRK's skyscraper and then the similar destruction of the seven palatial homes. They were secretly happy about it and publicly silent. They obviously couldn't say anything, except privately, and behind closed doors they all reveled in the fact that organized crime was getting its due, and all from one man, Natty Tracker. The government also secretly knew that the President of the United States would support Tracker as staunchly as he would the First Lady.

Natty then destroyed two homes that belonged

to Jaki Kurikawa and returned to Colorado Springs. He had no idea where she was, but he was more concerned with Yoshihisa and the other leaders of the RRK. Tracker decided he owed Doctor Kurikawa a personal debt, which he would settle at a later date. In the meantime, he would hit her and the RRK in the pocketbook as much as possible.

He was counter-attacking with a vengeance. Natty spent days in his computer room conducting an exhaustive search. After a week, he had located several RRK bank accounts set up in banks with dummy corporations.

The government had purchased several homes surrounding Natty's and Wally had sent a detachment from Fort Bragg's anti-terrorist Delta Force to stay with Natty and in the surrounding houses. The members of Delta Force had beards and civilian clothes and didn't look military, although they were chosen from the best of the best, so Tracker requested that he be allowed to let Dee stay there with him. His wish had been granted, and for him it had been a real *delight*.

Tracker called Wally Rampart on a safe phone and said, "General, is it possible to place a large amount of money into the US Treasury for a specific department?"

"Not really," the Undersecretary replied. "You can make donations to the government, but the money goes into the general fund for disbursement as deemed appropriate."

"Can I transfer money directly into that fund from various bank accounts?"

"I don't think so," the old war horse replied. "Why?"

"Because I'm going to be transferring millions of dollars in contributions to the US Treasury, but you need to arrange it so I can transfer it right into the account," Natty responded.

"I don't think so, but we'll set up a dummy account, and you can transfer funds into that, change the funds to cash, and donate it to the government," Wally said. "What do you want to call the organization and account?"

Tracker thought for a second and said, "Let's see. Let's name it the Strategic Harmony International Trust."

"Okay, sounds fine to me."

"Thanks, talk to you later."

Rampart interrupted, "Hey, wait a minute. How'd you come up with that name?"

Tracker chuckled and said, "Read the initials," and hung up.

Wally looked down at his notes and said aloud, "S-H-I-T," and laughed uproariously.

Tracker used his computers to analyze and discover the necessary access codes, and within a month started transferring funds from Green Lightning accounts to the account for Strategic Harmony International Trust.

He hired an old associate who had worked for the CIA for years as a pilot for Air America. He had retired after a nasty crash in Guatemala and was leaving the DC area. The man, Fletcher Harmon, took large amounts of money out of the SHIT account and hand-delivered it to the General Accounting Office. As far as the government was concerned, SHIT was a benevolent association set up to make contributions to the United States from wealthy benefactors.

Tracker also set up a meeting with executives and accountants from Dragon Lady Inc. in Las Vegas. The group had lunch at the new Rio Resort Casino and enjoyed the Brazilian atmosphere. Tracker had two phony executives with him who posed as an accountant and an attorney for his promising, but faltering, business. The non-existent business was actually a paper tiger created to attract Dragon Lady Inc. Tracker and the two phony executives with him—really retired cops with extensive experience investigating organized crime—painted a beautiful corporate picture with balance sheets, profit/loss statements, phony annual reports, and so on. They concocted a story about a small manufacturing concern that produced very inexpensive molded plastic coffins dressed up to look costly.

Tracker explained that he had started the company with money inherited from his father, an insurance executive who had immigrated from India and married an American woman who was a first cousin to the Rockefeller family.

Natty showed them a file full of phony court records and arrest reports with the story that he had "just played around" a few times with cocaine and had gotten busted. The fake records indicated that he had been busted dealing and had two prior convictions for possession and was facing serious jail time. He went on about how he needed money for his defense attorneys, but the Dragon Lady execs all gave each other knowing looks, thinking that he would use the money to skip the country.

They bit and asked what Natty wanted for the company lock, stock, and barrel. Tracker quoted a figure and then let them talk him down to one-sixth of his original price. They were on cloud nine when they wrote out a check for a cool one million dollars, and then at Natty's request cashed it and paid him in cash. His papers were ready to sign over, and he signed the whole business to them. Tracker left their offices two days after their first meeting. He carried a briefcase full of money and a big grin on his face, when he thought about Jaki Kurikawa finding out about their purchase of Green Lightning Casket Manufacturing, Limited.

Natty headed back toward Pike's Peak. He contacted Wally and let him know what had transpired and asked him to pull out all the stops in the intelligence and law enforcement communities to locate Yoshihisa Shibuya, Jaki Kurikawa, and other members of the Ryoku Rai Kyookai.

In the meantime, Natty sat at the computer and searched for credit card purchases, bank transactions, or anything else that could go into a computer that had RRK names attached to it, but apparently figuring he would be searching, they all had been using cash only. Tracker thought it would have to be that or they were all hiding out where money wouldn't be needed. Natty thought about it and figured that those

GREEN LIGHTNING

people wanted money and power for their own aggrandizement, so he couldn't see the entire group holing up and not spending money. He also couldn't picture them just spending small amounts of money; they were used to blowing large sums.

Knowing that Yoshihisa had a gambling problem, Natty kept feelers out in Vegas, Monaco, and Atlantic City.

Tracker had another thought and he started looking for something else in his computers. He then called friends at FBI headquarters in Washington.

Two days later, Natty received the call he had been waiting for. Pinehurst, North Carolina, contained the Golf Hall of Fame, and some of the finest golf courses in the world were there and at nearby Southern Pines. A high-roller Japanese golfer had been playing and betting heavily at the Country Club of North Carolina, Pinehurst Country Club, and several other major courses. Gambling wasn't officially allowed, but he was doing so much hustling that it was quite noticeable. He also was a heavy loser, and it seemed that the more he lost, the more he bet. Natty thought to himself: You son of a bitch. I look all over the world for you and you hide out in my own backyard.

The man went by the name of Ken Furoshiki. Tracker laughed to himself. He pictured looking at an obituary column in a newspaper and seeing two different obituaries for the same person.

Tracker had his specially made Stingray flown

by cargo plane to Pope Air Force Base at Fayetteville, North Carolina. He decided to wait and fly in the following day.

That night, Tracker slept fitfully and seemed to awake in the middle of the night. He felt next to him and Dee was not in the bed. He sat up in a fog and saw her walk out of the bathroom. Partially hidden in shadow, she appeared to be grinning and was holding something up in front of her. Natty switched on the bedside lamp and smiled at her. His smile turned to horror, however, as he saw the evil smile on her face and then saw that she held a straight razor in one hand: It was bloody. In the other hand, she held a bloody penis. Natty looked down and saw that his had been cut off. He looked up and Dee's face had changed; she was Henrietta Lynn James. He screamed.

"Natty! Natty!" Dee said, holding his sweaty shoulders as he sat bolt upright in bed. "Are you okay? You had a nightmare."

Tracker looked all around the room and gathered his wits. His heart was pounding, and he had broken out in heavy perspiration. He took a breath and lay back staring at the ceiling.

"You ever notice how James Bond goes through life—threatening situation after situation and keeps grinning and keeps wise-cracking?" he asked.

Dee smiled and said, "Yes, I have."

"Guess that only happens in books and movies, huh?"

She laughed. "Well, Natty Tracker, you mean to tell me that you're human like the rest of us?"

He chuckled. "I guess all grown men need to be scared little boys at times. I'm really glad you're here."

She stared into his light blue eyes and her heart fluttered like it always had. Tracker's dark complexion set off the sky-blue eyes with a startling contrast. He seemed to be able to bore right into her brain with those eyes, and they entranced her.

She caught her breath and said, "I'm very glad I'm here, too. You know, you don't ever have to worry about being a little boy. If ever there was a *man*, it's you."

Natty smiled and then got a sad, faraway look in his eyes.

"What's wrong?" she asked.

"Dee, you're too much of a woman. I was in love once before and she was killed. I vowed that I'd never again allow that to happen."

"Tracker, I know what you're saying. Let me explain myself, though. I don't want kids or a white picket fence. I love my job and I make good money with it. I also enjoy spending the money on vacations and excitement. You bring excitement into my life, Natty Tracker. I know you meet beautiful women all over the world, and I know what your life is like, but your life is so exciting, I can only take it in small doses. I enjoy that and can still enjoy my work as well. I don't want to own you, brand you, or bear your children. I want to share some quiet times, exciting times, and romantic times with you, and that's it."

He kissed her passionately and then she grinned at him and held her fist up to his chin.

She said, "Just remember, buddy. If you ever bring a disease to me, I'll make those ninjas look like Pee Wee Herman. Got it?"

Tracker laughed and kissed her again.

His F-15E Eagle touched down on the hot runway of Pope Air Force Base the next afternoon. He followed a dark blue pickup with government plates and a FOLLOW ME sign on the back. It led him to a hangar with armed guards around it, and he parked inside and then stepped into a black Cadillac limousine.

Less than half an hour later, he stepped out of the limo and walked up the old stone steps of a large building. Behind the building was a green golf course and in front a large sign reading OFFICERS OPEN MESS, MAIN CLUB, FORT BRAGG, NORTH CAROLINA. Inside Natty was taken to a table where Wally was seated eating a New York strip steak. He and Natty shook hands before Natty looked at the menu.

"Already ordered for you," Wally said with a mouthful of medium-rare steak. "Same thing. You'll like it. Good."

Natty grinned. "Thanks, I love steak."

Wally continued chewing and said, "Wife won't let me eat it at home. You know, cholesterol.

Every chance I get away, I order steak," he continued. "I like to just sit here and eat and then listen to my arteries slam shut."

Tracker laughed. "Why did you fly down here to meet me?"

Wally stopped eating and tapped the corners of his mouth with his napkin. He looked into Tracker's handsome organic/electronic eyes.

"Natty, I came to warn you," the old general said. "You've taken millions back from the RRK, and we have put them top priority for intelligence gathering. In short, they are pissed. We're getting reports back, and the word is that they're paying millions to make you very dead."

"Muammar Qadhafi put a bounty on my head and nothing's come of it," Tracker replied, unconcerned.

Wally responded, "You don't understand, man. There's an open contract out on you for millions of dollars. On top of that, our information is that they've recruited a high-priced army of thugs and hit men to kill you."

"That's not fair," Natty said, as he licked his lips over the juicy steak set down before him. "They need to get some reinforcements."

Wally started laughing. "Tracker, you're something else. You know, going after Shibuya could be a set-up. Why don't you come to Washington, or just let us beef up security at your place, and we'll pick him up?"

Tracker held up his hand. "And what if you can't make him tell you about the rest of the

RRK? You're restricted by laws in the way you deal with people like this. I'm not."

"That's true," Wally said. "That's one of the reasons we ask favors of you, an independent. Got word that he's got a tee-time tomorrow morning at 8:15 with two dentists and a local doctor who are pretty good scratch golfers."

"Great," Tracker replied with enthusiasm. "Where?"

"Pinehurst Country Club."

Because of newsmaking events after Ferdinand Marcos bilked the Philippine Treasury of billions for his own personal gain, and other foreigners carrying out similar acts, someone in the CIA got the idea to make short video tapes of wealthy foreign industrialists, bankers, and politicians. In case one of them was spotted with a known arms dealer or whatever, the file tapes could be used for easy documentation. It was a good idea since videotapes provided a more accurate identification of a person than photographs.

Tracker was looking down at a miniature television screen on his right wrist. Two fold-out black metal flaps shielded the glare from the morning sunshine as Natty looked at a videotape of Yoshihisa Shibuya taken one year before at an amateur tournament at Pebble Beach. Natty was glad that it showed him golfing, because he could positively identify him by his golf swing, walk, and mannerisms.

His eyes lifted from the tiny screen and he

GREEN LIGHTNING

zoomed his eyes in on the golfer who was teeing off. Hidden under an azalea bush, Natty couldn't be seen, but there was no doubt in his mind that he was now looking at Yoshihisa. Tracker lay flat under the bush while the foursome passed by, and then he moved to his hidden golf cart and went to another fairway.

Natty had picked out the rough along a fairway where there was a dogleg and good cover. Laying under some trees, he watched with his telephoto capability as Shibuya teed off and hooked his drive to the left of the dogleg. The ball landed out of sight of the golfers and only twenty feet from Natty. He ran out to the fairway and picked the ball up and looked at it. It was a black-lettered Titleist 1. Tracker reached into the cargo pocket of his trousers and pulled out several golf balls in a leather pouch with foam rubber-lined compartments. He saw a Dunlop Maxfli, an Acushnet, a red-letter Titleist, and then a black-letter Titleist. Natty pulled a stamp out of another pocket and an ink pad. He twisted a dial on the stamp and pressed it onto the pad. He then placed a number "1" underneath the name Titleist on both sides of the ball and set the ball down in the fairway.

Five minutes later, watching from back in the trees, Natty saw Shibuya and his opponents come into sight around the dogleg of the fairway. Shibuya spotted his ball and walked over to it after listening to the end of a dirty joke by one of the dentists. He looked at the green, some ninety yards distant, and selected a nine iron from his golf bag. He used the iron to slightly move the ball and make sure it was his ball. Satisfied, the Oriental duffer picked up some grass and let go of it, watching the way the wind blew it. He addressed the ball, took a clean practice swing next to it, lined up his shot, and swung.

With a loud *bang* and a big puff of powdery smoke the ball exploded, and the Japanese mobster fell to the ground, the wind knocked out of him by the concussion device. Tracker ran out from the trees as the other three golfers stared at him while getting up off the ground. They stood dumbfounded while they saw Natty handcuff Shibuya and gingerly pick him up and sling him over his shoulder. The gangster was conscious, but just barely. Tracker smiled at the men who now were trying to make weak protests as he carried the limp man toward the trees and in the direction of his hidden golf cart.

Natty waved, smiled, and said, "Don't worry, guys. We'll get him fixed up; his putter went limp!"

Tracker took off into the trees at a trot, as if he wasn't carrying anything. Reaching the cart, he took Shibuya to his hidden Corvette after giving the hood a shot of a powerful tranquilizer and muscle relaxant. He then left for his motel room in Southern Pines.

An hour later, Shibuya took sips of coffee while he sat at a table in Tracker's room. Natty stood across the room, double Glock 19s in shoulder holsters as he leaned against the dresser and faced his adversary.

GREEN LIGHTNING

Tracker said, "You saw what happened to The Shinkansen?"

"Yes," Shibuya replied.

Natty said "Do you need to go through a bunch of pain and torture, or do you want to save yourself the trouble and answer my questions now?"

It unnerved Natty when the Japanese henchman said, "I'll take the pain and torture."

Tracker would have expected an answer like that from Ken Furoshiki or even Jaki Kurikawa, but it didn't seem to fit the personality profile of Yoshihisa Shibuya. It puzzled Natty; the man was just too confident.

Tracker pulled out a gun and covered it and his hand with a sweater after slipping on a cotton sport coat. He helped the woozy gang boss out of the chair and stuck the hidden gun barrel against the man's spine. They walked to the door.

"Where are we going?" Shibuya asked.

Natty said, "Washington," and opened the door.

Shibuya stepped into the hallway and Natty followed but stopped short as he stared into the muzzles of ten automatic weapons held by Japanese henchmen, each dressed in a business suit and holding a briefcase in the other hand. One man retrieved his second gun, while the closest took the other from his hand. Natty grinned and raised his hands. A third man reached into Tracker's pocket and took out his car keys. He left the hallway as Natty was cuffed and Shibuya uncuffed. The tall American was escorted outside and into a big panel van. Inside the van, Natty was cuffed, arm and leg, into large steel braces welded to chains and bolted into the floor. Natty seemed to be helpless, with no hope for escape. He saw one man driving his Sting Ray in front, as two other men got into the front of the van and drove out of the parking lot. The other gunmen all climbed into the back with Natty and held guns on him.

The Corvette, followed by the van, pulled onto US Highway 1, crossed the center divider and turned south. The vehicles drove for less than twenty minutes and came to a small town called Hoffman. Right after Hoffman, they turned right and headed down a dirt road. Natty saw a sign that said SANDHILLS WILDLIFE REFUGE, NORTH CAROLINA DIVISION OF WILDLIFE. A few minutes later, both vehicles stopped at a nice little house in the woods, and he saw three men run into the house. Natty heard several short automatic weapons' bursts a few seconds later and the men ran out. He assumed it was the ranger's house.

The vehicles made several turns as they went farther into the sandy forest. White patches of sand abounded under stands of head-high scrub oaks that led into large stands of tall evergreens. There were also brushy fields of tall grass between the many patches of woods and scrub oak thickets.

Natty saw a deserted but well-maintained stable and a small frame building. A sign out front read NATIONAL FIELD TRIAL HEADQUARTERS, SANDHILLS WILDLIFE REFUGE, HOFFMAN, NORTH CAROLINA. Natty, with a good working knowledge of outdoor sporting events, knew this bobwhite and quail-laden reserve was where the proud owners and trainers of pointing dogs came with their horses to watch their animals work the fields and thickets. It was here that the national championships were held.

The field trial grounds, though, were now deserted, and Natty knew he was in serious trouble. Tracker saw the Corvette pull into a freshly bulldozed trench and the van followed it. The sound of a bulldozer starting up alarmed Natty, and he saw it appear at the trench's lip and push dirt over his customized Corvette. Natty had to control his heartbeat and breathing. He knew what was coming. All the hitmen exited the van and a smiling Yoshihisa Shibuya entered and sat down across from Tracker.

Yoshihisa said, "Stupid American, we caught you with one of your own tricks."

Natty interrupted, "You were wearing a transmitter?"

"Of course, you fool," the criminal said with much bravado. "Now, before I bury you alive and let you die slowly after you go insane from fear, I'll tell you a few things. Number one, I'm not the actual head of the Ryoku Rai Kyookai."

"Who is?" Tracker asked, not allowing himself to show the fear he felt.

"Jaki Kurikawa," the man said and let it sink in. "Her father had been in the Cherry Blossom Squadron."

"He was a kamikaze pilot?"

"Yes," Yoshihisa continued, "but the war

ended and he did not have to sacrifice his life. He became my aide, and I was very . . . a . . . aggressive in those days. I had a good business head and accumulated much wealth. Not everything I did was totally legal, and he kept notes. He used them later to blackmail me."

Natty interrupted with taunting laughter and Shibuya got very angry.

He continued, "I allowed the blackmail to continue because Kurikawa was a tough and clever adversary, but he was smart enough to not press me too hard, and I still have great wealth and power. His daughter, however, is much greedier and more power-hungry. She is much cleverer and more ruthless, but that will soon cost her her life. She has let me front as the head of the organization, but I also have control of all of our accounts. She's hard to kill, and I will only have one try, but it will work."

"No, it won't," Natty said with a grin. "Because I'm going to turn you over to Washington, so they can recover all the funds that have been stolen, and I'll kill her myself."

Shibuya laughed heartily. "You are crazy! There is no way you can escape. You will sit here in the dark and know that this van is covered with five feet of dirt, tons of it. The air will get thicker and thicker, until you will want to scream but will have no breath to do so. You will cry like a baby and wet yourself. You'll go mad from fear and frustration."

Natty stared at the Japanese punk. "No, I won't. I will escape and do exactly as I said."

GREEN LIGHTNING

Yoshihisa felt a cold chill run up and down his spine, but he forced a smile and said, "Well, Mr. Tracker, we will be up above in the sunshine camping out until you are very very dead, so if you escape, come and visit me."

Natty grinned, "I'll bring flowers."

Yoshihisa stood and exited the van and the bulldozer immediately started covering it with dirt. Tracker stayed calm and started thinking. His situation seemed hopeless, and he had no idea how he could possibly escape. Natty Tracker, however, had not grown up learning to be a quitter. If anybody could accomplish the impossible, it was Nathaniel Hawthorne Tracker, but how could he escape this predicament? Within minutes, the van was totally covered with dirt.

Yoshihisa Shibuya didn't know Natty saw with electronically enhanced eyesight, and he didn't know Natty was unscrewing the end of his left ring finger right now, using his other two fingers. The end of the finger fell off, and Tracker caught the scalpel and plastic ball in the palm of his hand. The radio antenna fell out of the finger's end as the tip rolled across the floor. Tracker yelled for Wally Rampart, but only got static; the metal van and the dirt interfered with reception. Natty was drenched with sweat already.

He decided right then that he would indeed escape, and he would invent a device to be added to the OPTIC System that would enable Wally, in Washington, to video-record and monitor anything Natty was looking at and hearing. He would, of course, figure out a simple way to start and stop the device. First, he had to escape somehow.

Tracker moved his left knee over and set the explosive ball down on it. He held the scalpel in his hand and positioned the keyhole of the iron left cuff over the ball on his knee. Natty carefully pushed up with his knee and the ball wedged halfway into the keyhole. The air was getting stuffy. He draped the left arm chain across his knee and held it in place with his right knee.

Natty Tracker gritted his teeth and slammed the cuff and ball down on the heavy chain. His head turned away, and he screamed in pain as the concussion broke his kneecap. It also shattered the inside of the cuff. The concussion didn't break the chain and fortunately only gave the kneecap a hairline fracture. Natty was also able to hold onto the scalpel. He used it to pick the lock on the right cuff, and it sprang free. He then picked the locks on the other two cuffs.

Tracker hobbled to the front of the van and opened the glove compartment. Inside, he found a thick road map and pulled it out. He pressed it hard against his broken knee and then wrapped his shirt around it. He removed his belt and wrapped it around the shirt, securing the splint with it.

Natty found a small screwdriver and used it to remove the screws in the plate at the top of the six-foot-tall chromed post that extended from the step in the front of the van up into the ceiling. In fifteen minutes, the post was loose and Tracker used it to break out the windshield on the left

GREEN LIGHTNING 167

side. Sand and dirt poured into the vehicle. Natty used the tube like a drill and extended it up through the dirt while it spilled out the bottom of it.

All of a sudden, a shaft of sunlight shot out the bottom of the tube and fresh air rushed in. Tracker stuck his lips to the tube and breathed in the air. He took breath after breath and then used a rag from under the driver's seat to secure the tube in place.

Next, Natty attached the end of the antenna wire to the tube's bottom and tried again to transmit. He got Wally Rampart on the radio immediately. Tracker quickly explained his predicament, and Wally told him not to worry. Tracker decided it would only make dirt cave in more if he tried to dig his way out through the windshield, and he also had no weapons to fight with against the many automatic weapons of his foes. He just breathed through the tube and listened through it. Wally called him to let him know help was on the way and kept other people on the radio talking to him to keep Natty from worrying about being buried alive.

Not much later, Natty heard what sounded like an AC-130 aircraft followed by loud shouts. Seconds later, Tracker heard what he felt were US Army Apache assault helicopters. He heard firing, screams, curses, and helicopter ordnance going off. Natty knew the Army had definitely arrived when he heard the sounds of battle.

Twenty minutes later, Tracker heard the bulldozer and saw the dirt above him being shoveled away. It took a full hour to get him out of the van, as soldiers had to dig him out by hand when the dozer got close enough to the van. Natty loved the daylight and fresh air. Army medics placed Natty on a stretcher and put a splint on his left knee. He looked around and saw many RRK assassins lying dead on the ground. There were Green Berets guarding RRK prisoners, including a wounded Yoshihisa Shibuya.

Ignoring protests, Natty got off the stretcher and walked toward Shibuya. The tall spy stopped and picked some wild flowers and handed them to Shibuya with a big smile.

Natty said, "I can help you with one goal, anyway. Where is Jaki Kurikawa?"

Shibuya smiled in defeat, "I wish I knew. I would love for you to kill her, but I do not know."

Tracker looked around and saw several Green Berets S-rolling parachutes and stuffing them into aviator kit bags.

Natty walked up to a master sergeant with a Special Forces patch on his right sleeve, indicating he had served with the Fifth Group in Vietnam.

"You guys jump in, top?" Natty asked.

The old NCO said, "Fuckin'-A. Got to kick some ass, too."

He walked off, giving orders to other men. Natty only saw one wounded soldier. Womack Army Hospital at nearby Fort Bragg would be informed that the man was injured in a training accident, which was the same story he would tell his family and friends. More ground vehicles and

GREEN LIGHTNING 169

helicopters arrived and soldiers were digging Natty's car and the van out. Natty walked over to a captain who was shouting orders.

Tracker said, "Captain, please thank your men for me, but I have to go right now. I need to borrow one of your choppers."

Ignoring the officer's protests, Tracker limped to a nearby LOH, light observation helicopter, got in, and took off. He flew directly to the hangar where his jet was guarded at Pope Air Force Base.

Five minutes later, Natty was airborne and headed for Washington, D.C. He called Wally to tell him he had to read everything there was on Jaki Kurikawa and find her. He thought she probably already knew the RRK was coming down around her ears and would take desperate measures. Natty was told to land at Dulles International Airport and a limousine would pick him up.

A short while later, Natty was dropped off directly in front of the US Capitol building and saw Wally Rampart and two members of the National Security Council as they walked down the steps. Wally waved at Tracker when he spotted him, and all of a sudden, Natty noticed the back of a woman tourist off to one side between him and Wally Rampart. She had shiny long black hair and was looking at Wally and hadn't seen Tracker. Her hair had been twisted on the back of her head into a tight, thick bun with two chopsticks sticking through it. She was reaching up and twisting the handle of one now. Natty yanked out one of his nine millimeters.

He yelled, "Doctor Kurikawa!"

Shocked, she turned and looked into Natty's eyes and the barrel of the polymer steel gun. A big smile spread across her face, and she pulled a thick file folder out of her over-the-shoulder bag. Behind her, Wally Rampart sat down on the step, his face ashen. His secret service agent/driver pulled out a MAC-11 machine pistol from under his coat, but Natty's hand came up in a halting gesture, and he dropped his arm.

She said cheerfully, "You won't shoot, Tracker."

"Why not?" he calmly asked.

"I know that you can shoot anybody and get out of it, but you are *too* moral. You're a law-and-order guy. Look, we even have a thick file on you, and look how I labeled it."

She held the thick manila folder up in front of her and in grease pencil on the front, was written N. H. TRACKER, ALL-AMERICAN HERO. Tracker smiled.

He said, "Doctor, you tried to kill our President. Why wouldn't I kill you?"

She smiled broadly and licked her full lips. "It's completely against your moral code. I'm unarmed. I'm a woman. I'm beautiful. You won't shoot. It would bother your conscience too much."

Natty looked over at Wally Rampart, grinned, and then looked at the beautiful woman again and said, "You used Henrietta James and stabbed me. You killed many and are very dangerous. You're a trained shrink and will probably plead insanity and get away with it, because you'll know how to walk the walk and talk the talk. It seems that you have declared war on my country. Are you really positive I won't shoot?"

She laughed and said, "Absolutely; it goes against everything you've ever stood for. It goes completely against your whole moral code."

Natty winked at her and said, "Wrong, Dragon Lady, I can live with it."

Tracker pulled the trigger, and a bullet passed through the "A" in Tracker's name on the file folder. She dropped the file and stared at the hole in the center of her chest in abject horror.

Jaki looked up at Natty with terror on her face and said, "You did it."

Her eyes rolled up in their sockets, and she fell on her face, dead.

Wally walked over and looked down at her body and said, "Lady, you didn't realize; you don't declare war on the ultimate warrior."

Henrietta Lynn James looked out the barred window of her asylum room and saw puppies playing together in the clouds. She stared.

Dee Light looked out the master bedroom window of Natty's mansion and wondered when he would return. She hoped it would be soon.

The President of the United States looked out an Oval Office window at the west lawn of the White House. He thought about the record-breaking period of peace and the many positive changes going on in the world. He thought about how peaceful things were and how big a landslide he would be reelected by.

The dreams and future of the Ryoku Rai Kyookai drained out through a hole in the chest of Doctor Jaki Kurikawa and spilled onto the steps of the US Capitol.